JUL 2 8 2012

HUNTER

ERIC WALTERS

ORCA BOOK PUBLISHERS

Library and Archives Canada Cataloguing in Publication

Walters, Eric, 1957-
Hunter / Eric Walters.

Issued also in electronic formats.
ISBN 978-1-4598-0157-8

I. Title.
PS8595.A598H85 2012   JC813'.54   C2012-901802-3

First published in the United States, 2012
Library of Congress Control Number: 2012935413

Summary: Hunter is a cat whose past has made him untrusting of humans,
but when his family is endangered, Hunter must put aside his fear and trust
a boy who has Hunter's and the cat colony's best interests in mind.

MIX
Paper from
responsible sources
FSC® C016245

*Orca Book Publishers is dedicated to preserving the environment and has printed
this book on paper certified by the Forest Stewardship Council®.*

Orca Book Publishers gratefully acknowledges the support for its publishing
programs provided by the following agencies: the Government of Canada
through the Canada Book Fund and the Canada Council for the Arts,
and the Province of British Columbia through the BC Arts Council
and the Book Publishing Tax Credit.

Design by Teresa Bubela
Cover photography by Getty Images and Corbis
Author photo by Sofia Kinachtchouk

ORCA BOOK PUBLISHERS
PO Box 5626, Stn. B
Victoria, BC Canada
V8R 6S4

ORCA BOOK PUBLISHERS
PO Box 468
Custer, WA USA
98240-0468

www.orcabook.com
Printed and bound in Canada.

15 14 13 12 • 4 3 2 1

To those people who care and provide
for wild cat colonies.

One

Hunter got up and stretched in a way that would make a yoga teacher jealous. He did a downward facing dog with much more grace than any dog ever could. He had been out all night hunting and had brought back a large mouse. It would have been enough for him. It wasn't enough for his mate, Mittens, and their brood of four kittens. He had taken a nibble, but most of it had gone to his family. The kittens mauled it more than they tried to eat it. They were still being nursed and were only just beginning to make the transition to eating meat. Until they could fend for themselves, Hunter would have to find more and more food for them.

He was a very good hunter—so good, in fact, that the other cats in the colony called him Hunter. If anybody could find food, it was him. He would have preferred to wait and go out at night, rather than in the middle of the day, but his stomach told him he needed to go out again, now.

In the evenings there was more prey out—mice and rats and careless birds that roosted where a cunning cat could catch them. At night Hunter's black fur blended into the darkness. Only the white star on his forehead was ever visible. And there were fewer *humans*. Humans were dangerous. They were the *most* dangerous. There was a cruelty to them he didn't understand. It wasn't their killing. It was that they killed but didn't consume. They didn't take a life to save their life. They didn't kill to eat. They didn't kill to survive. They just killed and left the body behind.

Humans roared around in loud, foul-smelling cars. At least the smell and the sound alerted animals to their approach. When the humans were inside a car, they were faster than any cat, faster than any animal, but they could be avoided by a smart cat. And he *was* a very smart cat. So smart he fed on the kills humans left on the roadside.

Quietly Hunter started up the hole. He tried not to disturb his family, but the four little kittens awoke and with them, their mother. The kittens rushed forward, head-bumping and playfully swatting and nibbling at him with sharp little teeth.

Being here with his little brood and their mother made Hunter happy. Happier than he'd ever been before. He had seen his share of hard times, but this warmth made up for it.

He scrambled up the incline of their den, followed by four little sets of legs. He stopped at the mouth of the den, and they bumped into him from behind. That's where they needed to be, not outside. He waited before exiting. He never left the den until he knew it was safe.

Before venturing out, he used his nose to search for danger. The smell of humans was always present. It filled the air, but as long as it wasn't too strong there was no danger. He turned his ears ever so slightly to the front and listened. As always, he heard the dull rumbling of street traffic from the other side of the fence.

Behind him the kittens pushed, trying to get out. He continued to block their way while his eyes adjusted to the daylight and he poked his head out the hole. On all sides he was comforted by familiar objects. Familiar was safe. New was potentially dangerous.

"It's safe," Hunter said. He stepped out of the hole and into the light. Immediately he was surrounded by the kittens, and their mother followed. "Have them stay close to the hole," he warned.

The kittens scrambled about, ignoring his words. He would have scolded them—or had their mother scold them—but there was no need. It *did* seem safe. They were surrounded by abandoned cars.

He thought it was strange how on the other side of the fence, cars were his greatest threat. But the cars in the junkyard, free of people and without their roar and rumbling, were harmless. The discarded cars provided Hunter, his family and the colony with protection, places to hide. The wrecks were everywhere, row after row, some stacked five or six cars high. A tall fence separated the junkyard from the road. Sometimes humans came into the junkyard, and occasionally dogs slipped through one of the holes in the fence. But for the most part, especially for a careful cat like Hunter, the colony was safe.

At a glance Hunter counted more than half a dozen other cats nearby. There were others that he couldn't see, but he could smell them. It was a big colony, and he knew every cat that belonged to it.

Some of the cats were awake and stirring, while others slept in the sun. Sitting on the roof of a wreck with the sun warming his fur was a favorite pastime. Especially since the cold and snow would arrive soon. He knew the winter was almost as dangerous as humans.

"Are you going to wait until it's dark?" Mittens asked.

"No. I need to go now."

"Be careful," Mittens said.

"Aren't I always?" he replied.

She nuzzled against him. He *was* careful. He was a good provider, a good father to her kittens, and if it weren't for King, he would have been leader of the colony.

Hunter looked around for King. He was nowhere to be seen. It seemed impossible for a cat as big as King to be invisible, but he was often out of sight. It was good he wasn't here now. He and Hunter left each other alone, but every now and again King let the others know he was still the biggest in the colony.

"Can we come along?" one of the kittens asked.

Hunter almost blurted out, "No!" But he held back. He didn't want to be rough with his kittens, as most of the tomcats were.

"Yeah, can we come? Please, can we come?" another kitten asked and others meowed in agreement.

"I will bring you all one day…but not *this* day…not yet. You're too small and your mother would be sad if you didn't stay here with her."

"Would you be sad?" one of the kittens asked their mother.

"Sad *and* worried," she said. "And you wouldn't want to worry me, would you?"

All four kittens hurried over and snuggled up against her.

"When you're older you will all come with me," Hunter said. "I'll teach you everything. You will become great hunters and—" He stopped midsentence.

"Get them below," he ordered.

Quickly Mittens gathered the kittens. They disappeared into the hole, and Hunter moved away from the den's entrance.

Thank goodness these humans were so loud. Their voices and footfalls echoed off the wrecks as they approached. Why were humans so noisy? They have no need to be quiet, thought Hunter. They have no enemies.

He headed into the wrecks, passing through a crevasse that was much too small for a human. From where Hunter was, he would be able to see the humans, but they couldn't see him. Their footfalls fell on the chipped cinder blocks.

There weren't many of them—two, perhaps three, four at most. They moved quickly, their voices soft, but their feet heavy. Their voices grew louder and louder until they rounded a wreck and came into view. There were two of them. Not old. This could mean mischief. The young ones, the human kittens, could either be good or bad. Better to prepare for the worst, he thought.

The humans stopped walking. One of them pointed at four cats lingering in the open. How could they be so unaware of the humans' arrival? Even a dog would have heard them coming and reacted.

The two young humans moved closer, stopped and slumped down, disappearing from Hunter's view. Although he couldn't see them, he knew where they were.

Carefully, staying in the shadows, moving through the wrecks, he circled the area until the humans came back into sight. They were focused on the four cats out in the clearing.

Humans didn't come into the junkyard often, but sometimes when they did they left food. Many of the cats scrambled after their food. Hunter never did. Not because he was too proud to take it, or too good a hunter to need handouts, but because he remembered. He *knew* the danger.

It happened a long time ago, when he was older than a kitten, but not yet a grown cat, in his old colony. He didn't like to think about it, but he remembered all the death. Almost every cat in the colony had died. Hunter fled, but he never forgot the deaths or the promise he had made.

He watched as the humans sat on the ground, talking and not moving. Their voices were gentle, not threatening. What were they doing? Strange. They weren't moving closer, but their scent increased. How could that be possible? Hunter's ears perked up. He tried to hear if more humans were coming. A tomcat slipped out from a gap between two wrecks. Didn't he hear them? Was he hoping the humans had brought food?

Then Mittens appeared with the four kittens following close behind. What was she doing? Hadn't she heard the humans? He rushed over to chase her away. A piece of brick flew through the air toward the cats and slammed against a wreck with a thunderous crash!

Two

Mittens and the kittens disappeared along with one of the four cats. The remaining cats were startled, but they didn't run and hide. The first two humans jumped up and spun around. Hunter froze. He crouched and fought every urge to flee. Three more humans, bigger ones, approached.

If two humans were dangerous, then five were even more dangerous. Humans were no different than dogs. They never hunted alone and instead traveled in packs. The five humans spoke. There was no telling what they might do next. Two of the newcomers clutched rocks in their hands.

Hunter thought about where to go if they directed their anger and rocks at him. He had an escape route to retreat to the den. It was important to have a getaway. But they weren't looking at him. If they wanted to harm cats, there were still three in the clearing. Hunter wondered what the boys were going to do next. He despised humans, but he was also fascinated by them. They were hunters, and he was a hunter. There was no danger in watching them if they didn't see him.

He couldn't understand what they were saying, but he could understand the anger in their voices and their bodies. All animals—cats, dogs, even humans— had a stance they held when they were about to fight. He had seen it many times before.

The first humans, the smaller ones, smelled of fear. It wasn't a pack of five humans. It was a pack of two and a pack of three. He was sure it wouldn't be long until the two fearful humans ran away. One of them started to edge away. He was getting ready to take off. Maybe the other three would chase him, or maybe they'd be satisfied that he had left. Another rock was tossed. It soared over the heads of the two smaller humans and landed on the ground, almost hitting one of the cats who hadn't fled. One of the smaller humans screamed out in anger.

Hunter remained still. Why had one of them screamed? Was he afraid the rock had been tossed at him? Was he upset a rock had been tossed at the cats? No, that couldn't be it. He was probably angry because he wanted to be the one to hurt the cats.

Despite rocks being tossed in their direction, the three cats in the clearing hadn't run off. In fact, two more cats had crept out of the wrecks, their curiosity trumping caution. They probably thought the people had food. Many of the cats were hungry. They didn't have the skills necessary to catch their own food, so they relied on handouts.

Suddenly one of the smaller humans bent down and picked up some rocks. His friend did the same. Were they going to start throwing rocks at the cats too? No, they were facing away from the cats. The two smaller humans were going to fight the other three!

Hunter had to admire them. Humans were his enemies and they were evil, but these two were brave.

The humans hurled angry sounds back and forth at each other. Hunter crept forward. They reminded him of barking, howling dogs. He loathed dogs almost as much as he loathed humans. He had heard stories about humans fighting among themselves, but he'd never seen it.

Something moved on the edge of the clearing. The human, the large man who lived in the junkyard, appeared from between two wrecks. He wore a cloth wrapped around his head and in his hand was a long club. The junkyard was his human den, and he guarded it well. He walked slowly forward. The two smaller humans were caught between him and the pack of three. They were so focused on the pack of three that they hadn't noticed the bigger danger behind them. The guard moved forward quietly. He was so quiet even Hunter could hardly hear his footsteps. Soon he would be on them. They were trapped and had no place to run.

The pack of three saw the large man approaching. They dropped their rocks and raced away. Hunter wasn't surprised. He had seen other humans run from the man before.

The two smaller humans turned around and jumped. It was too late. The guard was over top of them, ready to pounce. They were caught.

Three

The two smaller humans froze. The only chance they had at getting away was to run in different directions and hope that in the confusion the guard wouldn't know which one to chase. That's how Hunter avoided the dogs that occasionally entered the yard. If three cats ran in three directions, a dog would try to chase all of them and end up catching none. Even if a dog focused on one cat to chase, that still meant two were safe.

The two humans dropped their rocks. The guard was much bigger than them. He had darker skin and, as always, was wearing a cloth wrapped on his head. The humans were being submissive, probably hoping he'd leave them alone. Instead the guard reached out and grabbed one of them by the hand and gave it a shake! The guard did the same with the second person too. He grabbed him, shook his hand a little, and then he let it go.

Hunter noticed the guard's teeth were showing, a sign of aggression. Was the guard about to plunge his teeth into them and bite? No, he was being friendly. None of this made any sense to Hunter. He strained to hear what they said, but they were too quiet. That confirmed things. Humans were loud when they were angry and quiet when they weren't. They weren't going to fight. He watched as the three of them walked off and disappeared behind a row of wrecks.

Hunter got to his feet. He wasn't going to come out of hiding until he was certain they had gone. He crept forward. There was still a strong human scent in the air, but it was fading.

Hunter skirted around the edge of the clearing. He disliked the smell of humans even more than he did dogs. At least dogs always smelled like dogs. Not so with humans. Sometimes they smelled like food, other times like flowers.

Finally, coming full circle, he arrived at the entrance to his den. It was well hidden in the shadows and partially protected by an overhanging wreck.

He stopped at the entrance and looked around. He wanted to make sure he wasn't being observed before he went in. Satisfied, he disappeared down the hole. Mittens and their kittens were waiting for him. Before he could ask why she had brought them above ground, the kittens assaulted him. They were in a playful mood and didn't seem to understand what had happened out in the junkyard.

"I know what you're going to say," Mittens said.

"Have you become a mind reader?"

"I can read a mind when it thinks the same thing all the time. You're angry with me for appearing above ground when the humans were there."

He was, but he could never be angry with her for long. "You're free to do what you want."

"Of course I am. You don't *own* me."

Nobody could own a cat, especially a wild cat. But even more important, nobody could ever tell a cat what to do. They prided themselves on being independent and taking orders from no one, especially another cat.

"If you wanted to, you could have gone over and rubbed up against them," Hunter said.

"And if I had wanted to, that's what I would have done! I used to do that all the time," she said.

"Before they—" He stopped himself.

"Before they abandoned me?" she asked. "Is that what you were going to say?"

"I wasn't going to say anything."

"I wasn't afraid of them."

"Maybe you should have been *more* afraid of them."

"And maybe you should be *less* afraid of humans," she argued.

"Those humans were throwing rocks."

"Not the first two."

"They picked up rocks," he said.

She looked surprised. "They tossed rocks at cats?"

He wanted to lie and say yes. It would have made her more wary, kept her safer. But he didn't. "No," he admitted quietly.

"I knew they wouldn't try to harm us."

"They could have," he said.

"No, the first two people were safe. I could tell."

He knew she *was* probably right. Hunter knew about hunting, where to find food, how to avoid danger and where the best place to get out of the rain or cold was. But he didn't understand humans very well. Mittens did. He'd spent his life in the wild. She had lived the first part of her life with humans.

"Those first boys were not dangerous," she said.

Boys—what humans called their young when they weren't kittens any longer.

Part of him didn't even want to know what humans said. He had seen dogs on leashes, walking with humans, listening to their words and obeying their commands. It was almost as if their words were filled with power and control. But their words hadn't helped the dogs; they had only taken away their power.

Hunter wasn't some *dog*. He was a cat, a strong, powerful cat. If he could master the humans' language, maybe he could control them. Maybe he could walk them on a leash! That thought amused him. But he knew, even if he *could* put a human on a leash, he would never do it. Hunter valued freedom too much to take it away from anybody. Not even an enemy.

"I just need you to be careful," he said. "The kittens need you."

"They're not the only ones who need me," Mittens said, rubbing against him.

"I think it's the other way around," he replied. "You couldn't survive out here without me."

"I wouldn't *want* to survive out here without you."

She could be excused for saying something like that even though it was uncatlike. She had lived with humans for so long, she didn't understand how important independence was. Still, this cat that couldn't have survived without him made him happy. He didn't *need* her to survive, but his life had to be about more than just surviving. It had to be.

"The other boys, the bigger ones, I knew they were trouble," she said. "Even if they hadn't thrown that rock, I would have run."

"How did you know they were dangerous?"

"It was their faces," she said. "Humans are different than other animals."

"I'm not arguing that. What about their faces?"

"It was their expression. You know how a cat twitches its tail when it's angry?"

"Of course."

"And a dog wags its tail, when it's happy," she continued.

"Stupid dogs can't even get that right. But what does that have to do with faces?"

"Humans don't have tails so they show their feelings on their *faces*."

"Dogs and cats do that too," he said. "They snarl or show their fangs or hiss."

"But it's different. Sometimes humans show their teeth because they're happy."

"That makes no sense," Hunter snapped. "Why would you do that unless you were happy you were going to bite somebody…those humans are probably happy to bite anybody!"

"You know humans hardly ever bite," she said.

"That's because they have so many other ways to fight and hurt and kill, like with their cars."

"To know if a human is happy you have to look at their eyes and the curve of their mouths," she continued. "If the eyes get big, they are scared. If they get small they are angry. If the mouth curves up they are happy. If it curves down they are sad or angry or afraid or—"

"Why don't they just hiss," he said. "Wouldn't that be easier?"

"They do hiss," she said. "It's in the sound of their voices. Listen to the sounds."

"I know to run when I hear them coming, especially if they're loud."

"Loud can be bad, but so can quiet. You have to do more than *listen*; you have to *hear*."

"They are so loud. It's hard *not* to hear them."

"That's not what I mean," she said. She paused. "It's hard to explain, but I can just tell when they are angry, when they're dangerous."

"Aren't they always angry and dangerous?" he asked.

"Not always. My little girl was always nice." Mittens got that dreamy, lost look in her eyes. "She gave me food and milk, and scraps from the table. They tasted *so* good."

Probably better-tasting than what he brought to her, he thought.

"She let me lay down in a soft place, and it was always warm. She used to rub my fur…right behind the ear and—"

"It sounds like you'd rather be there than here," he snapped.

She didn't answer, which was, in its own way, an answer. He turned to walk away and she pounced on him, wrapping her front paws around his neck. He could have easily fought her off but he didn't. Besides, there was no danger. Mittens didn't have claws in her front paws. The humans she had lived with had taken them away. They had brought her to some place and put her to sleep. When she woke up, her claws were gone. It was another example of how evil humans were. Even the little girl Mittens spoke of so lovingly had been part of it.

Mittens started licking his head. Her rough tongue against his fur felt good. It reminded him of being a kitten, and of his mother. He had many memories of his mother. He didn't know his father, but he knew he must have been a fine hunter.

"You know this is where I want to be," she said. "There's no place I'd rather be than here with you and our kittens. My little girl never brought me mice like you do."

"Is that all I'm good for, bringing you mice?"

"Of course not. You bring me *birds* as well."

He knew she was joking, poking fun at him.

"I know these humans," she said. "You have to trust me."

"I trust you with my life," he said. "It's just that I don't trust you with *your* life. You're too valuable to lose."

She squeezed him even tighter and licked his fur even harder. "For such a tough tomcat, you certainly are sweet."

Here inside the den she could say things like that to him, but not in the junkyard, not in front of the other cats.

She started to purr. He loved the sound. It made him happy, so happy, that he made his own little purring sound. It was different from hers. She purred like a little motor. His was rough and rumbling.

"You know I only went up to look for food so you wouldn't have to go out searching during the day when it's more dangerous," she said.

"It's not that much more dangerous. Besides, I'm going to stay in the yard. I'm going to hunt in here."

She stopped grooming him and turned to look him in the eyes. "Those rats are dangerous."

"I don't understand how you're not afraid of humans twenty times bigger than you, but you are afraid of a rat."

"It's not *a* rat I'm afraid of," she said. "There are dozens and dozens of them."

"More than the paws of ten of us put together live here. Rats may live together, but they die alone."

"Couldn't you just wait until dark? Couldn't you wait until the birds start to roost?"

"I can wait," he said. "But the kittens can't, and neither can you. You need to eat to nurse them well. Don't worry. I'll be safe, and I'll be back. Now let go of my head."

"And if I don't?" she asked.

"Then you'll have to groom me a little bit longer."

Four

Hunter moved quietly, putting aside speed for stealth. There was no need for speed. The rats weren't going anywhere, at least until dark. He stayed off the ground, moving from one car to another. *Car*. What a strange human word.

He spent so much time around cars. They moved, made sounds and could take a life, but they neither ate nor were eaten. When their lives were over, humans abandoned them in the junkyard. Hunter jumped, cleared a large gap and silently landed on the roof of another car. He moved with grace and agility.

He wished Mittens didn't take the humans so casually. It made him shudder to think about what they'd done to her. A cat without claws was hardly a cat. Mittens was a cat, but she had been left so *vulnerable*. Without claws, a cat couldn't climb a tree to escape danger, defend itself or catch prey.

Almost without thinking, he flexed his front paws so his claws could extend out of their sheaths. It felt good. He was armed, dangerous and ready.

He knew that without him, Mittens couldn't survive in the wild. He tried to educate her, explain things, but she didn't always seem to understand. Perhaps it was the same as Hunter not understanding all the things humans said. Mittens didn't understand some things other colony cats seemed to know, even their kittens. Despite being declawed by her past owners and left to die on the street, she still had warm feelings for humans.

Of course Hunter had feelings too, feelings of anger, hate, disgust and distrust. If he had been bigger than the humans, he would have shown them what his claws could do. But even then, he suspected the humans would still have hurt him. They were evil, and they were clever.

Hunter had traveled almost the whole length of the yard without his paws touching the ground. He wasn't worried about his scent. He moved into the breeze, so he could smell what was in front of him, and nothing could tell he was coming. There were the usual odors: the car fumes, the powerful stink of humans, the smell of their food and, of course, the rats.

He did a little turn, looking in every direction. It was important to be wary. The hunter could quickly become the hunted. Satisfied, he started toward the ground. He was safer up in the wrecks, but there was no prey. Slowly, twisting through the remains of the cars, he wove lower and lower until he was just above the ground. From this vantage point he could pounce, hurtling himself down, claws extended and—

"I see you."

He looked over. There, poking his head out of a small gap was a very big brown rat, his fur glistening and his eyes glowing like two little embers.

"I see *you*," Hunter said.

"I could smell the *stink* of a cat long before I could see you."

Rats had noses that made cats seem like humans. A rat's sense of smell was so sensitive they never needed to ask one another where they'd been, who had been there, what they had eaten or if they were happy, sad, healthy or sick. All of that was obvious with just one breath, one sniff.

"You catch rats?" the rat asked Hunter.

"You know why I'm here," Hunter said.

The rat opened his mouth and showed his teeth. "Danger in catching rat."

"Dangerous for the rat."

"Clever cat want to eat a rat…want to eat *me*?"

"Not you," Hunter said. "You're too old and tough."

The rat made a rasping sound. He was laughing. "Many rats, but only one cat," the rat said.

"I only want one rat."

"Many rats with many teeth and many claws could kill a cat," the rat said.

"Call them out. Call them *all* out, so I can choose which one I want to eat."

"Maybe they will eat *you*."

"Then you better just bring one. Do you have one that *you* want eaten?"

"There are always many to eat. There are too many rats. Too many rats that want to be leader. *I* am leader."

"And I could help you remain leader…a leader with worn teeth and dull claws."

"Claws dull, mind sharp."

Rats were devious and clever, and this rat was more devious and cleverer than any other.

"You are a smart rat."

"A *very* smart rat."

"Am I your enemy?" Hunter asked.

"You enemy of all rats but *me*. You not enemy, you partner."

They *were* partners, or at least they had an agreement—an agreement that fed Hunter and eliminated troublesome rats from the rat colony. Rats live in groups, but they don't live *as* a group. No rat cared for any other rat. Even a mother would sacrifice her own pups if it meant escaping with her life. She could always have more pups, more than she could ever raise. There was no honor among rats.

"Go to the spot at the end of the path," the rat said. "I will bring him."

"I'll be waiting," said Hunter.

"I know."

Loudly, the rat screamed out something in rat that Hunter couldn't understand, but he knew the meaning.

Hunter turned and ran away. He had to put on a show, to keep the other rats believing their leader had scared him off. Hunter headed for their agreed spot. Hunter didn't trust the rat, and no rat ever trusted a cat. But they had come to an agreement, at least for now.

Hunter had to circle around and come to the meeting place from the far side, downwind, so no one would smell him coming.

As he crept through the junkyard, he thought about the rat. He was *king* of the rats and evil, but also clever.

He'd lived longer and ruled longer than any rat should. Rats ruled by fear and force, tooth and nail. But this rat was well beyond physically holding off his competition. He had held on to his position by being more clever and devious.

He approached the designated spot and found his familiar perch. He was no more than three feet above ground and was sheltered by a wreck. He was hidden from all sides. There was a clear path straight down to the ground. He could make a swift jump onto anything that passed below. And something *would* pass. Soon.

He turned his head, listening. He knew it wouldn't be long. His mind went blank. There was no need for thought. He worked on instinct. He flexed his paws, exposing the claws, testing them. His muscles tensed and relaxed. He was ready to pounce. His ears flattened back and his pupils dilated. A rat appeared below, running through the gap. Hunter hurled himself on it, crushing it with his full weight. His claws pinned and pierced it. The rat was lifeless beneath him.

He heard scratching and spun around. A dozen or more rats armed with sharp teeth and claws were behind him. He hissed and they fled, running back into the wrecks.

"No honor," he said. "Just rats."

Five

It was a big rat. So big Hunter considered stopping and eating some of it before carrying it the rest of the way back to his den.

He approached the colony. Already he could sense several cats nearby. He knew he would have an audience when he arrived. That was fine. That was good. To bring back his catch for all to see only confirmed his status as the best hunter in the colony. A rat was a formidable opponent, especially one this big. But he *was* Hunter. Only a skilled hunter, a *brave* hunter would even attempt to take on a rat.

Normally he weaved through the wrecks, staying under them, but not today. It was such an impressive kill he wanted everybody to see it. He had a swagger in his step as he came into the open space at the center of the colony. Instantly the other cats took notice of him. They were impressed. Some of them got up, stretched and came toward him for a closer look.

"That's quite the catch," one of the tomcats said.

Hunter stopped and set the rat down on the ground, placing a front paw on top of it.

"He's enormous," a younger cat added. "Did he put up a good fight?"

"Does it look like he put up a good fight?" Hunter asked.

Mittens came out of the den and approached Hunter. They touched noses. "You're all right...right?" she asked.

"Do you think a little rat could harm Hunter?"

"It's not such a little rat," a calico cat said. "It looks so big it could be king of the rat colony."

"It *is* big," a voice said.

Hunter didn't need to turn around to know who the voice belonged to. It was King, the old tom and leader of the colony. He was standing off to the side of the colony.

King was the largest cat in the colony. He was bigger than Hunter, bigger than any other cat in the colony, which was why he was the King. He was white and gray, and one ear was ripped and torn from a long-ago-forgotten fight. Often he seemed to be slow-moving, but in an instant he could pounce and attack, quick as lightning. Over the years, he had chased away cats that challenged his position. Those that remained were forced to accept their place beneath him. Every cat in the colony was beneath him, except Hunter.

Hunter had never confronted King, and King had never confronted Hunter. Occasionally Hunter would secretly bring King some of his kills, to pay homage. But since the birth of the kittens, Hunter hadn't been able to kill much for King.

"The rat is big enough for a king to eat," King said.

Hunter had known this would happen someday. He just wished it wasn't today. Maybe it didn't have to be. King slowly moved toward Hunter. Hunter felt his fight-or-flight senses activate. If he fled, he'd leave behind his kill and lose face in front of the other cats, in front of Mittens. If he fought him, he couldn't possibly win, but he could put up a good fight.

Hunter didn't know he wasn't the only one who wanted to avoid a confrontation. King knew he was bigger than Hunter. He was confident in his strength and skills, and he was an experienced fighter. But there was something about Hunter that unnerved him. King knew he would win a fight with Hunter, but he wondered what the cost would be. Would he be hurt in the fight? If nothing else, chasing Hunter away would cost him future meals. Right now he would bide his time and wait.

"The big ones aren't very tasty," King said. "Too tough."

King walked off, leaving Hunter with his foot still firmly planted on top of the rat. Hunter picked up the rat and started toward his den. He wasn't going to give King a chance to change his mind. He ducked down the hole with Mittens behind him.

Instantly he was swarmed by the kittens. He dropped the rat and they converged on it. He retreated to a corner of the den.

"I hate him," Mittens said.

"You and most of the cats in the colony."

"If everybody feels that way, then why *is* he the king?" she asked.

He shook his head. "It isn't a popularity contest. He's the king because he is the biggest and the best fighter."

"If he had attacked you, I would have fought him," she said.

"What?"

"I would have attacked him," she said.

"Don't even talk like that. You can't fight him."

"Is it because I don't have front claws?" she asked.

He didn't answer.

"I still have my teeth. I could dig them into his neck and—"

"Have you *ever* been in a fight?"

"Well, when I was a kitten with my litter mates."

"That's play. Have you ever seen King fight?"

"I see him bat around the other cats all the time," she said.

"No, I mean a *real* fight. One where he uses his fangs, claws and weight. He is a savage."

"I don't care how savage he is. I wouldn't stand by and let him—"

"If I ever have to fight him, I don't want you to stick around. I want you to run back to the den, to take care of yourself and our kittens."

"I couldn't do that."

"You have to," he said. "Look, I have avoided fighting him, but sooner or later it's going to happen."

"And that's when you'll need my help."

"You couldn't help me."

"What if a few cats all attacked him at once?" she asked. "Not just you and me, but some of the other cats who he's hurt or stolen food from or was mean to in the past?"

There was so much she didn't understand. "That's how dogs fight," he said.

"Everybody says you'll be the king someday."

"Talk like that is going to get me into a fight with him."

"You would be a better king than him. You would take care of the other cats the way you take care of me and our kittens. You would give them guidance and teach them how to hunt."

"That will never happen," he said. "That isn't how cats operate. You know cats never tell each other what to do."

"Why not?"

"Cats are too independent. We're not dogs," he said.

"Then maybe we should learn to be a little bit more like dogs."

"Don't be silly. There's nothing we could ever learn from dogs except how to drool and smell bad."

She went over and nuzzled against him. "You *will* be a good king."

Hunter didn't answer, but he didn't disagree.

Six

King sat in the middle of the junkyard's clearing. He soaked in the last rays of the setting sun. Hunter kept an eye on him as he circled the edge of the clearing. That was how it worked. Neither of them said anything or looked at each other. Whenever their paths crossed, King stayed on the ground and Hunter wove up along the top of the wrecks.

There was no point in confronting King. Hunter couldn't win, at least not yet. He would wait, bide his time. As King got older, Hunter would only get stronger and bigger. Time was his ally.

Cats living together weren't like humans, dogs or rats living together. Humans liked democracy.

Dogs favored dictators. They *liked* somebody to tell them what to do. And rats were fascists, brutal and uncaring of each other.

Cats were anarchists. They preferred disorganization, no hierarchy and no rules. Cats would never tell each other what to do. So getting a group of cats to work together was nearly impossible. Their mantra was *Independence, free thinking and free acting*.

Dogs ran and hunted in packs. Rats were always together, crowded so close together it was hard to tell where one started and the other ended. But not cats. They were too independent. They hunted by themselves. They fought by themselves.

King was the leader of the colony, but that didn't mean he led. He wasn't wise, caring or compassionate. He didn't take care of the other cats. He was the biggest, the most feared, and because of that he got what he wanted. He could decide to sit, sleep or nest wherever he desired. He had his choice of mates, and most importantly, he got first choice of any food Hunter brought back. King decided who could live in the colony. If he didn't want somebody there, he drove them away with his fangs, claws and fury.

When Hunter first arrived at the colony, he had to have King's permission to stay. He made sure King knew he wasn't going to be a threat, so he brought him a mouse he had caught, and gave it to him at their first meeting.

King got up and jumped onto the hood of a car. He followed the trail of the setting sun and soaked up the last few rays of warmth. The other cats were becoming more active. He wouldn't be the only one heading out to hunt. It was time for Hunter to leave, and getting the first kill was the best guarantee of a successful night.

Of all the cats, King was perhaps the least catlike. He was so big, so overstuffed, that he seemed to waddle rather than slink. Leaping up onto the hood of a car was almost the limit of his athletic ability. Hunter knew if a fight developed—*when* a fight developed—between them, his ability to move quickly would be his only advantage. If King pinned him down, he would rip Hunter to shreds. Hunter would have to make sure any fight with King occurred out in the open, so he had room to pounce and get out of the way. He wondered if King thought about their eventual confrontation as much as he did.

Hunter looked over toward his den. Mittens was there, surrounded by the kittens, a blur of movement, running, rolling, fighting and falling over each other.

She was a good mother. He cared for her, cared for their kittens, maybe more than a tomcat should. And there was really only one way to show them how he felt. It was time to go on the hunt.

Seven

Hunter slipped out through a hole in the junkyard's fence. There were more holes than he could count. He made a point of never using the same one twice in a row or twice in the same week. Habit made creatures predictable and vulnerable to enemies.

He stopped, looked around and listened to the low rumble of the cars in the distance. There was nothing concerning, nothing out of place. Hunter exited the junkyard. The wind blew into his face. Smells filled his nose and brain. The stink of cars and humans dominated. That wasn't the scent he sought. He closed his eyes, and other smells surfaced. A whiff of dog

was present. Hunter thought dogs stank. Sometimes
their scent became so intertwined with the humans they
blurred together. He could also smell skunk, other cats,
raccoons and mice.

As the night approached, the streetlights would
come on. They were so strong, they seemed to turn
night into day. Hunter had learned over time that
humans needed lights to see at night. They weren't
capable of seeing in the dark. Not like a cat. That always
made Hunter feel superior...but also vulnerable.
How could you fight an enemy that could turn night
into day? They were as powerful as they were evil.

He started down the alley. It was darker there.
He moved slowly, trying to stay in the shadows at
the edge of the alley. It was better to stay out of sight,
hidden from his prey.

There were always mice where humans lived. Mice
squeezed through tiny openings and made themselves
invisible. They lived on the crumbs and droppings
humans left behind. Food spilled out of human's buildings and overflowed from their garbage cans. Rats,
mice, raccoons, skunks, cats and the occasional stray
dog dined on the remains.

Hunter preferred to catch and kill his own meals.
Seeing his prey alive meant it was healthy, that it wasn't
tainted or—

Hunter froze. Footsteps approached. Human footsteps that scuffed along the pavement.

Silently he moved behind a garbage can. The wall of the building pressed against him. He positioned between the garbage can and the wall so he could peek out and watch the approaching human. He smelled the stink of a dog. A human and a dog tethered to it with a piece of rope appeared. A dog off leash might have been able to detect Hunter and come after him, but the leash restrained him.

The human couldn't smell or hear Hunter either. But he might see him. The safe thing for Hunter to do would be to pull back his head so he'd be hidden. But he didn't.

The dog strained at the leash. Hunter couldn't imagine a cat being walked, or any other animal for that matter. A rat, raccoon or skunk would never permit themselves to be walked.

The human yelled, and the dog stopped and dropped to the ground. When the human grunted, the dog got to its feet and walked beside him. Hunter watched this routine a half a dozen times. Was the human punishing the dog, or simply showing him who was in charge? If the dog didn't respond instantly, the human gave a sharp tug at the leash and the dog whimpered in pain. Hunter could almost feel the leash around his own neck, digging in, stopping him from breathing. He almost felt sorry for the dog.

Hunter moved around the garbage can, but he was still able to see. The dog dropped onto its haunches when the human yelled out, "Sit!" The dog got to its feet and walked beside the human when it said, "Heel." No cat would heel, even if it was dragged along by a leash. It would fight every step, scratch at the human, tear at the leash. Even Mittens, who had lived in a human den, had never been put on a leash. Cats could be contained. They could be captured or killed, but they would never walk beside a human like a mindless dog.

The human yelled at the dog one more time, and again it dropped. The human bent down and rubbed his hand against the dog's head. Hunter knew about this. It was a form of grooming. It was the same thing cats did to each other with their tongues. Humans used their hands. Mittens had told him about the girl she used to live with who spent hours patting her. Even to this day, Mittens would sometimes close her eyes and glow, when she remembered being rubbed behind the ears by the girl.

He watched the dog press against the human's hand and close its eyes. It looked as if the dog enjoyed what was going on. In a few seconds it had gone from being tortured to being rewarded. If Hunter had been tugged around on a leash, he would have tried to scratch the human's eyes out. But for the dog the pain was forgotten.

The human and dog both got to their feet and started off. Hunter wondered: What would it be like to have a human scratch behind his ears? The question disturbed him more than it brought comfort. He hoped he never got close enough to a human to find out.

Eight

It had taken a while for the alley to return to normal. The dog and human had chased away all the prey with their clumsy presence, loud voices and heavy footfalls. Slowly the mice returned and came out of hiding. Hunter spotted a plump mouse and moved in for the kill. He crept up and pounced on it. It was dead before it even realized it was in danger. This one was bigger than the first mouse Hunter had caught earlier that day, which was good for the kittens, but not necessarily good for King. He had given King his first kill to appease him, making himself seem useful and putting off their eventual confrontation. Now was not the time for a fight. Not when Mittens and the kittens needed him.

Hunter hurried back to the colony. Tonight he wouldn't go hungry.

Other toms made sure they had their fill before they shared a kill, if they ever did share. Toms were not known for their sacrifices to their families. But mothers were another matter. Not only would they hurl themselves against a big dog to defend their litters, but they also nursed their young at the expense of their own health. Hunter had seen more than one mother waste away until there was nothing more of her left to give and no way to recover. He would never let that happen with Mittens. She was a good mate and so defenseless, so helpless, without him. He would never abandon her or allow her to be hurt or abused. He suspected any future confrontation with King would involve Mittens. Eventually King was going to hurt her, or want to take her as his mate. King knew Hunter wouldn't allow that to happen. So he stayed away, for now.

Hunter entered the clearing. The scent was familiar and reassuring. Cats—lots of cats—lounged on the ground and on the tops of the cars. They were waking from their catnaps and getting ready to go hunting. Hunter froze. The big human who was always in the junkyard and someone else whose scent was familiar stood at the edge of the clearing.

Hunter hoped they wouldn't see him. But they turned and one of them extended an arm, pointing. He had been spotted. Quickly Hunter backed up and headed through a gap in the wrecks. He circled around, darting in between the wrecks toward his den.

Hunter didn't like to be surprised. Why hadn't he seen, heard or smelled the humans? He thought through the reasons. They were standing very still, and their voices were low. They were hidden behind the wrecks, so he couldn't see them. The wind was coming from behind him as he entered the clearing, making it impossible for him to pick up their scent.

He looked around. He was still hidden from view by some of the stacked cars. He couldn't see the humans, and they couldn't see him. Quickly he circled the last wreck, the one shielding his den, and disappeared into the hole.

The kittens swarmed him. He resisted the urge to give them a swat, so he could have some space—spare the paw, spoil the kitten. He dropped the mouse, and the kittens pushed and pulled and shoved at each other and the mouse.

"There are humans up there," he said to Mittens.

"Yes, it's the boy from the other day with the big man, the guard who is always here."

"Best to keep the kittens inside."

She nodded. "Probably best, but I don't think he means any harm. Maybe we should go up. Maybe there will be food."

"I *brought* food."

His feelings were hurt, and she knew it. She nuzzled against him. "You didn't just bring food, you brought better food. I'm sure he doesn't have a mouse up there. But still, we should go up."

He turned to the kittens. "You four stay here, or you'll be getting a swat so hard you'll be knocked into yesterday. Understand?"

The kittens stopped and meowed out agreement before they started brawling over the mouse again. He hoped it would keep them amused and underground for a while longer.

Hunter led the way up the hole, stopping at the entrance. It was just as important not to be seen exiting the den as it was not to be seen entering. He smelled, listened and then tentatively peeked out. He could hear voices in the distance, and there was a faint human smell. He left, followed quickly by Mittens. He started off, as always, in a direction perpendicular to the way they wanted to go. It was never wise to show your trail. Wordlessly, Mittens followed. She never questioned his way of doing things when it came to safety.

Hunter curved around the wrecks, moving through small spaces that provided shelter, safety and secrecy. He knew the nooks and crannies of the cars so well he could have moved through them with his eyes closed. He came out at the edge of the clearing, but he was shielded beneath a wreck.

The two humans were still at the far side. A number of cats were lounging, sitting, standing and waiting close by. Between them and the humans was King. He crouched in the middle of the clearing with his tail swishing back and forth as if it had a life of its own. He was staring at the humans. Hunter couldn't see his eyes, but he knew they would be burning intensely.

Hunter admired King. It wasn't smart to sit in the open, to not take shelter, but it was brave. King wasn't backing down. He sat there, suspicious and vicious, ready to act. Hunter knew if King was confronted, he wouldn't retreat. He had seen him stand up to humans before. He would puff up his fur, so he looked larger than he was. He would hiss and snarl and show his fangs. Hunter had even seen humans back away from him.

At first glance, a person might have thought King was defending the other cats, putting himself between them and danger. That wasn't the case. King would fight, but only to defend himself. He was there because he was curious, and he could smell food.

"Do you think they're dangerous?" Mittens asked.

"Humans can always be dangerous," Hunter said. "But their voices are quiet and that is good."

"Remember, humans can sound one way and act another. They can lie with their voices," Mittens said.

"They have food. I can smell it," he added.

"But humans always have food. So far they haven't shared it," she said.

"Well, they're standing still."

"They are, but that could be a lie too, designed to pull you closer before they strike."

Hunter had seen that before. "They are *such* good liars," he said. "Not like cats. A cat hisses when it's angry, crouches before it pounces. Cats are honest."

"Humans are skilled liars, but they can't lie with their eyes."

"Their eyes?"

"It is the way to see inside of them. You can tell if they are honest or angry, happy or sad, friendly or about to become a foe," she said.

"But if you can see their eyes, then they can see *you*," Hunter said. The thought sent a shudder through Hunter's body.

"Yes, but that's the only way to truly tell," Mittens said.

It was unavoidable to come in close contact with humans, but to look at one was dangerous. Cats hardly ever looked directly into one another's eyes, and when they did it was seen as a challenge. Wouldn't that be the same with humans? Would they consider it to be a challenge?

King glared at the humans. Hunter admired his bravery.

"Look," Mittens said. "They have food."

The boy had opened a bag and pulled out some food. Hunter couldn't tell what kind of food—it was something new to him. The smell wafted across the clearing, drawing more cats into the clearing.

The boy tossed a piece of food toward King. King jumped up, faster than somebody his size should have been able to, and knocked it out of the air and to his feet. He whisked it into his mouth.

The boy scattered a handful of food across the clearing. Several cats scrambled after it. Mittens shot past Hunter. He almost called her back, but he knew he couldn't stop her. As Hunter watched, Mittens grabbed a scrap of food. He could only hope it wasn't tainted.

The big man now pulled out food and threw it toward the cats. More and more cats came out of hiding to join those already feeding.

Hunter couldn't help but think back to a time long ago, when he wasn't much older than a kitten. Humans scattered food among his old colony. All of the cats, including his mother, had fed greedily, gobbling up the food. Hunter kept to the side and hadn't eaten anything.

Hunter had been so angry. Other kittens, some even younger than him, had been allowed to scamper after the scraps. Why had his mother kept him from eating it, even though she was? And then over the next two days, he had begun to understand.

It started with the biggest cats, the toms and the leaders, who had eaten the most food. They were the first to die. It happened quickly, but not quickly enough. They died, screaming in agony, curling up into balls or twisting in pain and throwing themselves about. They became raving, convulsing demons who couldn't communicate. And then they were still, silent, dead.

Hunter's mother wasn't affected right away. She was old, so old her last litter had only produced one kitten. She hadn't been able to get more than one or two pieces of the scattered food. But then it started. At first it wasn't severe. And then gradually the discomfort grew to pain, agony and ultimately death. In the end, his mother wanted to die to be free of the pain. Before she passed away, she asked Hunter to promise to leave their colony and to never eat food from human hands. He scavenged and took what humans discarded, but to eat the food they offered was another matter.

As the only kitten in his mother's last litter, Hunter and his mother had a bond closer than most mothers had with their kittens. They had spent a lot of time together. She was a wise mother. She explained things to Hunter, told him stories about cats, rats, dogs and humans. Hunter learned how to hunt from his mother.

In the end, it was easy to keep his promise to his mother because there was no colony left to leave. All but two other cats had died. Nothing remained but memories. Hunter feared the humans would return, so he left.

He lived on the streets for months, moving from one place to another, dodging humans, cars and dogs. He had quickly learned how to survive. But he missed living in a colony. He missed being with other cats, and so he sought a new colony to join. King hadn't exactly welcomed him, but he hadn't chased him away either.

The second promise he had made to his mother was harder to keep, especially when food from humans was offered so willingly. But so far, he had kept his word. He ate the food left behind by humans. There were never enough mice, rats or birds for the cats to survive on alone. But he always remained cautious and ate the bits and pieces and scraps he found in alleys.

Protected under the overhang of a wreck, Hunter watched as almost half the cats in the colony ate the scattered food. He had to trust Mittens was right: the food wasn't tainted. And in all likelihood, it wasn't. Many times humans had offered food to the colony. Never had the food caused a death. At least not yet. Still, he had given his word. Others could eat, but he could not.

If he was king of the colony, he would have tried to stop the other cats. But no king could control a whole colony, no matter how strong he was, or how much they feared him. And it would have been wrong to try. Not only would it have defied the cats' independence, but without taking the humans' handouts, most of the cats in the colony could never survive.

Suddenly King rushed forward, causing cats to scurry out of his way. One cat didn't move fast enough, and King swatted him on the side of the head, a powerful blow that sent the young cat sprawling. King snatched the scrap of food the smaller cat had been eating.

Mittens joined Hunter's side. "He is such a bully," she said.

"He's the king."

"You're not going to be that way when you're king, are you?" she asked.

"That's how kings always are," he said.

"Because that's how they *are* doesn't mean that's how they *have* to be. You *could* be different. You *are* different."

"How am I different?"

"The way you treat me and our kittens. If you treated everyone that way, can you imagine what our colony would be like? Cats looking after cats, working together and—"

"It sounds more like you're describing a pack of dogs instead of a colony of cats."

"Well, if that's what dogs are like, then maybe we should try to be more doglike."

"Keep your voice down," he hissed. "You don't want others to hear you talk like that. What would they think?"

"I don't care what they think," she snapped. "I only care what you think."

"I think that next time you'll be suggesting we act more like rats or mice or even humans," he said.

"We could learn from all of them."

"We're *cats!*"

"Does that mean we're perfect? Does that mean we can't learn to be better? Does that mean we can't—?"

"Enough!" he said, silencing her. "The humans have gone, and I have to leave too. There is still hunting to be done."

Nine

Hunter moved silently along the deserted street, staying in the shadows. It was never completely dark in the city. Lights were always present—if not from the cars, then from the windows of the humans' dens or the tops of poles. Humans didn't like darkness. He knew their eyes did not see well in the dark, and the lights helped overcome that weakness. Humans didn't seem to like darkness. Hunter thought they might even fear it.

He had watched from the shadows as humans walked by at night. The confidence, the strut with which they moved during the day was absent, especially when they were alone. They looked as if they were being hunted, rather than being the hunters. The only thing they had to fear was other humans. They must be like cats, thought Hunter. The little ones are afraid of the big ones, the young are afraid of the old, and the weak are afraid of the strong.

At dusk, there were almost as many humans and cars as there were during the day. But the later it got, the less there were, until by the middle of the night they were rarely seen outside. Hunter could hear them talking inside their dens, and flashes of headlights passed now and then, but the streets were basically empty, left to the cats, rats and other night-roaming animals. Most nights he saw more skunks, raccoons or possums than humans. While none of them were friends, neither were they enemies. But everyone kept a wary eye on each other.

Occasionally a dog or two would appear. They were nothing more than an annoyance to Hunter. Their senses were so dull that if he didn't move, they often walked right by him. Even if they had noticed him, dogs weren't equipped to climb, so a leap over a fence or up into a tree provided Hunter with all the safety he needed. Hunter had always chosen flight over fight, when possible. A wary cat, and Hunter was always careful, could sense their approach. Between their loud footfalls, their jangling chains and their heavy breathing, dogs were impossible to miss.

Hunter had only been cornered by a dog once. Fighting it had been his only option. But dogs were badly equipped fighters. Having their only weapon— their teeth—located beside their eyes had ill prepared dogs to scrap with cats. A determined cat, showing fang and claw, could keep a dog at bay. A lightning-quick claw to the face or a dog's muzzle would send it whimpering and yelping as it ran away.

But a pack could be dangerous. As a group, their puny brains and lack of confidence were lethal. Hunter had heard stories about packs of dogs catching a cat. They would attack from all directions, nipping and biting, spinning the poor cat around until finally one dog would rush forward and chomp down, killing it. Then they would tear it apart, leaving fur, blood and guts on the ground. Like the humans in their cars, dogs didn't always kill for food, they just killed. Hunter thought dogs had spent so much time with humans that they had adopted some of their most *disgusting* habits.

Hunter slipped under a fence and pressed his body against a human den. There was no sound and only a little bit of light coming from one of the windows. Even when they slept they had to have lights on. It was as if they were afraid of being swallowed up by darkness. Hunter thought he might have felt the same way if his eyes were dull.

He caught sight of movement above and froze. It was a cat on a windowsill, illuminated by the light coming from within the human's den. Hunter was surprised the cat had gotten this close without him noticing sooner. He should have picked up its scent before now. Unless…the cat was inside the den, behind the glass.

Using all of his senses, Hunter surveyed his surroundings. He was alone—except for the cat inside the den. It was looking at him. Effortlessly, Hunter jumped up to the narrow window ledge. The cat inside jumped slightly backward. Its reaction was neither quick nor graceful, hardly catlike at all.

Slowly Hunter lifted a paw and tapped the window. He looked through the window and at the cat. It stared back. Hunter couldn't tell if the cat was a tom or a she-cat because he couldn't pick up a scent through the glass, but he had nothing to fear—it wasn't a very big cat.

"Hello," Hunter said. "It is a nice night to catch a mouse."

The cat didn't answer. Couldn't it hear him?

"I'm Hunter!" he said, much louder.

The cat didn't answer, but slowly, cautiously, it inched forward.

"Can you hear me?" Hunter asked.

"Hear, yes," the cat said. "Why?"

"Why…why what?"

"Why you here?" it asked.

"I'm here to say hello," Hunter said. "Just being friendly."

"You no friend."

Hunter turned his head to the side. What was wrong with this cat? Why was it talking so strangely? It was like a kitten who hadn't learned to speak properly yet.

"No share food. Food is *mine*," it said.

"I'm not here for your food," Hunter said.

"Go away!" the cat hissed.

Instinctively the fur on Hunter's back bristled, making him look bigger than he was. The little cat sprung forward and banged against the glass with a loud thud. Hunter struck back, swatting the glass.

They screeched and hissed at each other. A bright light came on inside the house. The humans were awake. Hunter should have fled, but he didn't. He wasn't prepared to leave this fight yet.

"Someday, when you're outside, I'll find you, and there will be no window to protect you," he said. "But not this day."

He jumped down from the ledge and disappeared into the darkness. Stupid cat. Stupid humans. If he ever did find that cat outside, he'd give it a lesson on manners. But he didn't have time to think about it any longer. He was still hungry. He turned and headed toward the bridge where he knew there might be some pigeons that hadn't chosen a safe place to roost for the night.

Ten

The feathers tickled his throat as he carried the pigeon back to the junkyard. Despite the feathers, he liked bird much more than rat or mouse. He fought off the urge to stop and eat it himself. He wasn't going to do that. He would share it with Mittens and the kittens.

The kittens were growing fast. Some of the older she-cats had warned him against mating with a house cat. They didn't think Mittens would have the skills necessary to raise a litter. But Mittens was a great mother. Their kittens weren't just growing bigger, they were growing smarter. And they were respectful, as much as kittens could be. They stayed silent and listened when they should. And remained in the den when it was dangerous.

They were old enough now to move around independently outside the den. They pestered Hunter to take them with him on his hunting trips. But that was impossible. They were still too young, too noisy and clumsy to catch anything except unwanted attention. When they were older he would bring them with him. He wanted to pass on his hunting skills. It would be better for them to be taught by their father than to have to learn how to hunt on their own.

Hunter slipped through a hole in the fence and entered the junkyard. He was safe—well, at least safer. Bad things could happen in the junkyard, but they were more likely to happen outside the yard. He headed straight for the colony. Another time he might have skirted around in the yard and come in from the far side so he wouldn't attract looks from the other cats who wanted to see, or take, what he had caught. The only one who could threaten him was King. But even King wouldn't bother Hunter tonight. He was too well fed.

For weeks, the boy, and some others his size and smell, had been coming to the yard on a regular basis. Sometimes it seemed like they were there every day. They didn't bring a lot of food, but there was enough to feed a few cats, and sometimes there was even enough to feed all of them. The first helping always belonged to King. It was as if the boy knew. He always threw the first piece of food in King's direction. Even a human could recognize a leader. With King fed, he was less of a threat. He would still bully the other cats to get more than his share, but he was far less likely to chase after Hunter and claim his kills.

Hunter cut through the clearing. The other cats noted his catch. He slowed down and adjusted his grip on the pigeon, so more of it was visible.

He knew many of the cats admired his hunting prowess. But he had also heard grumbles from other cats about how silly it was of him to go out and hunt when food was being delivered to their colony almost daily. Nobody had said anything to his face. Aside from King, no cat in the colony was more respected, or feared, than Hunter.

Mittens was sitting at the entrance to their den. Her kittens surrounded her. They were so busy chasing and fighting over a piece of paper blowing in the wind that they didn't notice their father approach. He dropped the pigeon and announced his presence. Instantly they abandoned the paper chase and charged toward him, bumping into and tripping on each other. Hunter stepped aside. It wouldn't be very becoming to have them knock him down.

They tore into the bird, gagging on feathers. The interest and eyes of other cats were drawn toward the action. A couple of cats edged forward. Hunter stopped them with a glance. This wasn't their kill and nobody was going to bully his kittens, unless... He thought about what he would do if King came out and tried to take the pigeon? What would he do if King swatted at his kittens? Would he sit there and watch him, or walk away? He knew what Mittens would do. She'd hurl herself at King, and then there would be no choice. Maybe if Hunter came from the side and hit him hard enough, King wouldn't even see him coming. Hunter would have to make that first shot a good one, because he might not get a second.

Anxiously he looked around for King. He was nowhere to be seen. Thank goodness. Maybe he should shoo the kittens into the den so they'd be out of sight.

"They're very hungry," Mittens said.

"It's for you too."

"I'm okay...I'm not hungry."

"Was the boy here this morning?" Hunter asked.

"No. He usually doesn't come until later."

"You won't need to eat his food. I brought you food. Better food."

"It's all right to eat the food he brings. He's a *good* human."

"You told me even a good human can do bad things. Why take chances when you already have food?"

"You're right," she said. "It's just…just…"

"Just what?"

"It's just that he reminds me of my little girl, the one who cared for me."

"You mean the one who abandoned you and left you to die?" he snapped.

He regretted his words instantly. Mittens turned and walked away.

Eleven

Hunter not only heard them approach, he felt them. The footfalls on the ground sent vibrations through the soil. There were humans up top—more than one. His instinctual response was to stay in the den, away from prying eyes and human harm, but he couldn't. Mittens and the kittens were above ground.

Quickly, but carefully, he went to the mouth of their burrow. There was no point in giving away its location. If the humans knew where it was, it would be dangerous for the kittens.

The smell of the humans was strong, even before he reached the entrance. He peeked out. There was no sign of anyone, and their voices weren't too close.

He exited and dashed in the opposite direction of the voices. They seemed to be coming from the clearing.

Moving with speed, stealth and silence, he snaked through the wrecks until he reached the edge of the clearing. He was careful to stay within the shadows of an overhanging car piled on top of another. He didn't have to search to find the humans. There were several of them. He counted eight altogether.

Humans all looked pretty much the same, but he recognized the boy and the man with the cloth on his head. Seeing them there was reassuring. They had never harmed the cats. But what did the others want? Why were they here? The boy stood near Hunter. Was it Hunter's imagination or did the boy come closer to the center of the clearing each time he visited? The other humans hung back, standing at the edge of the clearing. They seemed fearful. Were they afraid of the cats or of the boy? Was the boy powerful?

The boy pulled out some food and made a high-pitched sound that stung Hunter's ears but got the attention of all the cats. The smell was strong and unmistakable. It was a bird...*chicken*. Yes, it was chicken! It was strangely reassuring to know humans liked to eat birds too. Hunter thought any animal that liked to eat birds might have some good qualities.

He wondered how they felt about rats and mice. Did they eat those too?

The smell filled the entire colony. Hunter felt himself drool, like some sort of stupid dog. The scent was so strong he felt like it could have pulled him out of his hiding spot. It *did* pull other cats closer. King, who had been sitting on the hood of a car, jumped onto the ground and approached the boy. Other cats were drawn in too. Seven or eight cats gathered around the boy.

Was this part of his plan? Had he been feeding the cats so that they'd become trusting of humans, so they'd come so close that the other humans could pounce on them? No, the others stood too far back.

Hunter saw Mittens and their kittens among the feeding cats. The kittens stayed close to their mother, but she was very close to the boy, separated only by King and a few cat lengths. He wanted to tell them to leave, warn them, drive them away, but there was nothing he could do now.

The boy tossed the first piece of chicken directly at King, who dove at it.

Then the boy tossed food around the clearing. It was as if a spark had been thrown on a bonfire. The whole space ignited with cats scrambling for the scraps. Mittens and the kittens were among them.

There was a frenzy of feeding, but there was so much food there was no fighting. There seemed to be enough for everybody.

Hunter startled as the other humans moved forward quickly. Were they going to pounce on the cats now that they were distracted? No, they pulled out more food and tossed it to the cats. The boy had brought several other boys and a girl, and they all had food for the cats.

The humans seemed happy. Their voices were high and they showed their teeth. Hunter still didn't think that it was a good sign. But as they stood around tossing food, not rocks, and feeding the cats instead of hurting them, Hunter decided Mittens must be right.

Part of Hunter wanted to join the other cats as he watched them eat. But he was a hunter. He didn't have to depend on handouts from humans.

King charged at three teenage cats. Two of them scrambled out of his way, but a third didn't move fast enough. King cuffed him on the side of the head, and the small cat tumbled over, rolling and then getting up and running away. That was one lesson the small cat would probably never need to be taught again. He should have kept his senses about him, been aware of King's approach. King had the right to do whatever he wanted because he was the king.

Hunter thought about battling King. Sooner or later it would happen. But as long as the boy kept bringing food to the colony, it would happen later, much later.

Hunter looked up and was shocked to find the boy looking directly at him. Cat and human locked eyes. Hunter wanted to stare him down, but he didn't. The boy's eyes were soft, gentle and caring. He looked directly into the boy's eyes. It was true: the boy wasn't going to hurt the cats.

Twelve

Hunter never felt so alive as when he was on the hunt. That night his senses tingled as he moved down the alley. It wasn't quite dark, so he stayed close to buildings and stayed in the shadows. As far as he could tell, there was nothing else in the alley—no cats, humans or even rats—but it was hard to know for sure. The alley was filled with smells. There were so many and they were so strong, they almost blinded his nose. But if he couldn't smell anything, neither could the rats or mice he was hunting.

Two large, loud exhaust fans forced more fumes out of a building and into the alley. At times, the noise was even more pervasive than the smells. Hunter had to rely on his sight. As darkness continued to unfold, his night vision was his best tool…and his best defense.

The hunter could always become the hunted, so he had to be wary. In the alley there were hardly ever any cars. And humans rarely walked down it, especially at night. He knew they were inside the buildings, but other than opening a door to bring out garbage, he hardly ever saw them here. Sometimes a door would be left propped open. He was careful around these openings, but he also peered inside sometimes. Curiosity with a *purpose*. He wanted to find out more about the humans. While he knew he'd never share Mittens's feelings for them, he did find them fascinating. They were hunters like him, but also organizers and builders. They were ruthless, but they were successful. They were the dominant creature.

He snaked around garbage cans, threading his way through the small gaps and openings where his prey might be hiding. He stopped to feed on crumbs that had spilled out of the cans and then continued. At each twist he was ready to pounce. But at each twist there was nothing. Maybe he needed a different vantage point.

He leaped up onto a row of garbage cans. Their lids were sealed tight, some were even held in place with cords. Even through the lids he could smell the food inside. This food wasn't something that was being thrown to him, like charity. This food he took was food he had hunted for. Since humans didn't intend for him to have this food, he knew it was safe.

Unfortunately his paws and claws couldn't open the containers. He had to wait for a can with a lid that had been left open or tipped over and the contents spilled out onto the pavement. He prowled the alley, looking for rodents and garbage. In one way, the two weren't much different: He couldn't catch a mouse that wasn't there, and he couldn't eat from a can that wasn't open.

Up on the garbage cans he had a better view, and he was safer. With height came advantage—something no dog could ever understand. Dogs were such limited animals. They couldn't climb or imagine.

From this elevation, he could pounce on an object below using gravity and the force of his weight, to add to the might of his muscle and the speed of his attack. Most animals didn't look up, so an attack from above was much more of a suprise. Hunter had learned to look side to side, up and down when he was on the prowl.

Once he had been hunting in a field and stalked a mouse. Slowly, stealthily, he had crept closer and closer to it. He had placed himself between the mouse and its hole. There was no place for it to run. He crept closer and closer. Ten lengths away, then nine. The mouse still hadn't seen Hunter, but then a bird swooped down from the sky and grabbed it.

Hunter had been so startled he jumped backward. The bird flew away, carrying the mouse in its claws. Hunter had been close enough to hear the bird's talons sinking into the mouse. He had been angry with the bird. But there was nothing he could do. It wasn't as if he could grow wings and chase after the bird.

Many times since that day Hunter has seen hawks kill. They were fast, faster than any cat, and moved on silent wings, more silent than any cat could be. For the first time he actually questioned whether another animal might be superior to cats, but dismissed the thought. Sometimes he wished he could fly. He almost *could* fly. He leaped up from the cans and landed on a window ledge, far above the garbage bins.

His body tingled and he froze. Cats had an extra sense, one Hunter doubted even hawks had. They could see things beyond their vision and hear things that barely made a sound. Slowly, first with his eyes and then with his head, he scanned the surroundings. He saw movement. It wasn't much more than a darker patch, more a shadow than an object, and it was moving.

He narrowed his eyes and focused on the shadow. It was big, at least three times as big as him, and walked on all fours. Was it a dog? He was safe on the window ledge. He wouldn't be noticed. The animal shifted and came toward him. It was neither graceful nor quick, and it waddled. He knew it was a raccoon.

The raccoon emerged from the shadows. He was brown and black. He was big, much bigger than most of the raccoons Hunter had seen.

The raccoon slowly made his way forward. They were awkward creatures, but they had sharp claws and teeth, and could climb. Hunter had heard stories about raccoons confronting dogs and sending them howling. Cats and raccoons tended to leave each other alone. Raccoons didn't prey on cats, and cats couldn't prey on raccoons. A cat could kill a raccoon kitten, but it would be risky. Raccoons were protective and aggressive parents. Both the mother and the father helped raise a litter, just as Hunter and Mittens did.

At first the other toms in Hunter's colony had grumbled about his role as a parent. "Tomcats don't act like mother cats," they had said. But after Hunter attacked the big tabby who had questioned him, he never heard about it again.

The raccoon rumbled forward, stood on his back legs and leaned against one of the garbage bins. The raccoon was so big his head peeked over the lid. He used his front paws to try to pry off the lid. Hunter was fascinated by the raccoon's paws. They looked like human hands more than animal paws. Those little fingers worked independently to try to unpeel the lid. The raccoon tried and tried, but it wasn't working.

The raccoon wrapped his arms around the can and rocked it, back and forth. It swayed and crashed to the ground, making a tremendous noise. Hunter was afraid the noise had attracted the attention of humans. He looked around, but no one entered the alley.

The can was on its side, but the lid remained in place. The raccoon wasn't through with it yet. He worked on the lid until it popped open and garbage spilled out.

The can was filled with food, and Hunter was hungry. Hunter got off his haunches and slowly moved forward. He wanted what was inside the can, and he was going to get it.

The raccoon had his back turned to Hunter and was focused on the food. Hunter slinked along the length of the ledge and leaped on top of one of the bins. He landed as softly as possible, and the sound was muffled by the drone of exhaust fans attached to some of the buildings.

Hunter crept along the tops of the bins. And then the raccoon saw him. The raccoon stopped feeding and the two animals locked eyes. He opened his mouth. Hunter saw a glint of white and knew he should retreat. But instead he leaped to the ground, giving up the only advantage he had—elevation. He crept forward, closer and closer, finally freezing only a few lengths away from the raccoon.

The raccoon didn't move to attack, and he certainly wasn't running away. Instead, he leaned into the garbage can, pulled out a piece of food and tossed it toward Hunter. It landed at Hunter's feet.

"Thank you," Hunter said.

"You are welcome, my friend. I thought you weren't going to come," said the raccoon.

"I thought *you* weren't coming," Hunter said. "If I could have opened up the can, I would have started eating without you."

"Instead you practiced your catlike stealth. Even for a cat you're particularly stealthy."

"High praise."

Hunter sniffed the food and began eating. He heard a sound, a human sound. Hunter looked all around. The raccoon turned and looked in the same direction. They both saw the human hiding in the bushes on the other side of the alley at the same time. He wasn't very big, just a boy.

The boy stepped out of the shadows, and Hunter recognized him. It was the boy from the junkyard, the one who had been feeding the colony. The two animals stared at him and then the boy spoke. His voice was loud enough to be heard over the exhaust fans, but soft enough not to be a threat. The boy showed his teeth and made a sound—laughter, Mittens had called it. It was a sign he was happy.

"We don't have to be afraid of him," Hunter said.

"Yes, I know. He's going to go now," the raccoon said.

As the raccoon predicted, the boy stepped into the alley and walked away, disappearing from sight.

"How did you know he was leaving?" Hunter asked.

"He said so."

"You understand human?" Hunter asked.

"I've learned to understand some of what they say. But how did *you* know he meant no harm? You don't trust humans."

"I know that boy."

"Don't you see humans as enemies?" the raccoon asked.

"Yes, don't you?" Hunter asked.

"I'm eating their food. Their junkyard provides shelter for you and your colony. Do enemies provide food and shelter?"

"Do friends kill and poison?" Hunter said.

"I didn't say friends. Just not enemies," the raccoon said. "Can't there be something between friends and enemies?"

Hunter didn't know how to answer.

"Take cats and raccoons. We're not enemies, but we're not friends," said the raccoon.

"Oh, I thought that…"

"*We* are friends," the raccoon said. "You and I, but usually cats and raccoons are not friends."

"Why are we friends?" Hunter asked.

"Let me tell you about my mother. She was killed by a car."

"I told you humans are our enemies!" Hunter snapped.

The raccoon shook his head. "The car and the humans in it were not trying to kill my mother. It just happened. It was an accident."

"It happens too often to be an accident. They are trying to kill us."

"No, if they were trying to kill us, then we would be dead," the raccoon said. He reached into the can and pulled out another piece of food, tossing it to Hunter. "I sat on the road, beside the body of my mother for a long time. I was alone, and so young that I didn't know what I should be afraid of. Other cars came by, but ignored me. Then a big mother cat appeared." He paused. "Looking back at it now, I think she may have thought about eating me."

"Cats don't eat raccoons," Hunter said.

"Only because they can't. Wouldn't you have tried to kill me the first time we met if I wasn't so much bigger than you?"

Hunter didn't answer. He *was* a cat, so that thought had entered his mind.

"I was so little, that the mother cat could have killed me. In some ways it would have been more kind to kill me than to leave me there to die. But instead she took me into her den. The reason I am friends with you is that my life was saved by a cat…a cat who reminds me of you. I think of us as brothers."

"I've never had a brother or a sister. I was the only one in my litter. But if I did have a brother, I could do no better than you," Hunter said.

"That is a high compliment. I believe in my next lifetime I may even come back as a cat."

"I don't understand. What do you mean, come back as a cat?" Hunter asked.

"It's hard to explain. I'm not sure what I mean myself, but I'll try. Someday we will all stop living, but I wonder if after this life we might come back in another form."

"I still don't know what you mean," Hunter said.

"Something about us, our *essence*, is more than just the body we live in. When the body stops, I think the essence goes somewhere else. Maybe into a kitten being born, or a human or even a dog."

"I'd never want to be a dog!" Hunter said.

"Most of them are harmless, simple sorts who just follow orders. At least the ones I've talked to."

"You talk to dogs?"

"Yes, they mainly talk about food, listening to orders, and for some strange reason they often talk about squirrels."

"Squirrels?" Hunter asked.

"They are *fascinated* by squirrels."

"What could you ever learn from a dog except how to drool and scratch yourself?"

"There are many dog qualities I admire. They are loyal, and they take care of each other. Can you imagine how a cat colony would work if cats could be counted on to care for each other?"

Hunter had been thinking about that ever since Mittens first mentioned the idea to him. But he knew it wasn't possible. He was surpised to hear the raccoon talking about it too. "Cats are too independent to follow orders or work as a group," said Hunter.

"Aren't you and Mittens working as a group of two to raise your kittens?" the raccoon asked.

"That's different."

"Not really. Two is just a smaller group. The two of you remind me of a pair of geese more than a couple of cats."

"Do you see any feathers?" Hunter asked as he lifted up his paw.

"No, but I do see a couple dedicated to each other. Do you know geese mate for life?"

Hunter shook his head. "I didn't, but I'd like to talk to a pigeon one day."

"Very dull birds. They make dogs seem bright."

"I only want to tell them to land on the ground where I can catch them." Hunter laughed.

"You'd be surprised. It's very hard to kill something you've spoken to. It's hard to hate something after you see how connected we all are," the raccoon said.

"Cats have to kill to live. Besides, if we come back as something else after we die I'm doing a rat a favor killing it so it has a chance to come back as something better."

"A rat might not see it that way," the raccoon said. "It's been so long since I took another creature's life."

"We kill to live," Hunter said.

"That is part of being a cat. That is a big part of your essence," the raccoon said. "That cannot be changed, but you could learn so much from other animals. The faithfulness of geese, the loyalty of dogs, the organization of humans, the cleverness of raccoons, the—"

"The stink of skunks," Hunter said.

"Okay, perhaps not all animals. But I know you'll be wise enough when you're king to—"

"What makes you think I'll be king?" Hunter asked.

"You will be," the raccoon said. His words were quiet, reassuring and certain. "I like cats, but not *all* cats. In fact, if I ever decide to kill anything again, I'll walk into your colony and gut that king of yours. He's not a nice fellow."

"He doesn't need to be nice, he's the king."

"But he could be nice, if he wanted to. One day you'll be a different sort of king." He reached into the can and pulled out another piece of food and threw it to Hunter. "But until then, keep learning. There is much to learn."

Thirteen

Hunter tilted his head to the side. He heard something coming. He hoped it would be the raccoon, returning again to meet him in the alley today. Then he heard voices. It was humans. He slipped behind a garbage bin. They were getting closer, louder. There were two, maybe three, humans. Then he recognized one of the voices. It was the boy. And with him was a female human who was bigger than the boy. Hunter suspected it was the boy's mother. His friend, the raccoon, had explained that humans raise their young for years and years.

The boy led her forward. The mother's voice was soft and quiet, but there was something about the way she moved that made him think that she was uneasy. Hunter smelled food and wondered if they were heading to the colony. They continued down the alley. They would have to take the long way around to a hole in the junkyard fence that was large enough for them to pass through. As soon as they were out of sight, Hunter ran across the width of the alley and underneath a fence. He wanted to be waiting for them when they reached the clearing.

Hunter had seen the boy almost every day. Either early in the morning or later in the day, before sunset. Always he had food with him. Always he gave it to the cats. And always he was kind and gentle. Hunter was still wary of him, but he was starting to trust him, just a little. And while the trust was only growing slightly, his fascination was growing by bounds. Hunter often stayed off to the side, watching and listening to the boy.

Hunter slipped between the parked cars. He wanted to get to the colony before them, so he could sit and watch them but not be seen.

He heard a scream, a human scream. Hunter froze. Before he could react, the raccoon came scampering toward him.

"I didn't know you could run that fast," Hunter said.

"Neither did I," the raccoon admitted. "I guess I just needed the right encouragement. I almost ran into two humans."

"The boy and his mother."

"Did you see me run by them?" the raccoon asked.

"I saw them in the alley and thought they were headed for the yard. That's where I'm going." He paused. "Would you like to come with me?"

"To where the humans are going? I think I've been close enough to those humans already. Shouldn't we both be moving in the other direction?" the raccoon asked.

"No, I need to get close enough to see what they're doing."

"Because you don't trust them?"

"Because I need to *learn* from them…and you could help me."

"I'll go with you as long as we don't get too close."

"We'll be off to the side so they won't see us," Hunter said.

"Good. I don't want to startle them again. People are often afraid of raccoons."

"I wish they were more afraid of cats," Hunter said.

"No, you don't. If they're afraid of you, they would hunt you and kill you," the raccoon said.

"They kill cats all the time with their cars."

"I told you, they don't do it on purpose. Those deaths are because they don't see us. They kill animals they are afraid of. That's why there are no bigger animals where they live, where we live."

"There are animals bigger than humans?" Hunter asked in amazement.

"Much bigger."

"And you've seen them?" Hunter questioned.

"I know of them. Someday I'll show you what I have seen."

That thought sent a tingle through his cat senses. He wasn't sure he wanted to see an animal that humans were afraid of and was bigger than him.

"Now let's go and look at the humans," the raccoon said. "They're scary enough."

Hunter led and the raccoon followed. The raccoon could not move as quickly or quietly as Hunter. He grunted and had to force his way through some of the narrower passages. Finally they circled around, skirting through the wrecks to Hunter's hiding spot. They climbed underneath a car and were hidden. Nothing could attack them and they had lots of ways to escape.

They could hear the humans. Strange, even with his pace slowed by the raccoon, Hunter should have been able to get here before them. He cautiously poked his head out to look. There were humans, but it wasn't the humans he had expected! There were three grown humans, and they were surrounded by dozens of cats. Hunter looked for Mittens or the kittens and—

The boy ran toward the humans, screaming and yelling at the top of his lungs as he charged at them!

Fourteen

The three others staggered backward. They're afraid of the boy, Hunter thought. But why would they be afraid of him? They are all bigger than the boy.

The boy continued to yell. The man tried to speak, but the boy cut him off. His voice was loud and angry. The man cowered away from him. The boy must be a brave and ferocious fighter, thought Hunter.

The boy ran past them and charged at the cats that were out in the open. The cats ran away, disappearing into the wrecks. Why was he after the cats? He had never harmed them before. What was the boy doing? Had Hunter misjudged him, was he no better than the other humans?

All of the cats had left, except for King. He stood in the center of the clearing. He wasn't going to give up his meal without a fight. King stood his ground, hovering over the food he had been eating, unwilling to leave it behind. A couple of the other cats hissed at the boy before they ran off. But King didn't hiss. He just glared and puffed up his fur to make himself look even bigger. He was an *impressive* king.

"He is so brave," Hunter said, under his breath.

"I don't think it's that he's brave. He's hungry and greedy," the raccoon said.

"He's standing up for what is his," Hunter said.

"He's standing up for his food. Defending his food makes him greedy. Defending other cats would make him brave."

"Still, he's not running away."

The boy screamed at King and moved toward him. King didn't back away.

"He *is* brave," Hunter said.

The boy bent down and picked up a rock. He heaved it toward King, barely missing him. King jumped in the air, turned and ran away, disappearing into the wrecks.

"How could I be so wrong about that boy?" Hunter said.

"What do you mean?" the raccoon asked.

"He's like all the rest. He just wants to harm the cats. He's no better than those other boys who throw rocks. He was only pretending to be our friend so he could trick us."

"No," the raccoon said. "You're wrong."

"I saw it with my own eyes. He chased them away when they were feeding. He even tossed a rock at King."

"I've thought about tossing a rock at King myself," the raccoon said. "You're wrong about the boy."

"You saw what he did, so how can you argue?" Hunter demanded.

"We both saw what he did, but I think you don't understand *why* he did what he did. He wasn't trying to harm any of the cats. He was trying to protect them."

"By throwing rocks and chasing them away?" Hunter asked.

"He was protecting them by chasing them away. That's why he ran at them, and that's why he threw a rock at King. He didn't hit him."

"Just because he didn't hit him doesn't mean he wasn't trying to—"

"Silence!" the raccoon hissed, showing his teeth.

Maybe the boy wasn't the only one who had fooled Hunter into thinking he was a friend.

"Be silent," the raccoon said. "I want to hear what they're saying."

The humans were yelling. The boy was yelling the loudest.

"What are they—?"

"Quiet," the raccoon snapped.

The boy stood his ground. He stepped forward, forcing the three others to back away and cower from his advance. Hunter understood. This boy was a warrior. But why would they be afraid of him? And how could the raccoon think he was good after he had attacked the other cats?

"Ah, that's makes sense. That is why," the raccoon said.

Hunter wanted to ask what made sense, but he knew to stay silent. He had respect for the raccoon, and a healthy dose of fear. He didn't want those teeth and claws turned on him.

"The boy acted as he did to defend the cats," the raccoon said. "He chased them away because he thought the other humans meant them harm."

That made sense. Perfect sense. There were times when Hunter had wanted to chase Mittens and the kittens away when he felt they were in danger.

"The rock he threw was meant to only chase King away. He was trying to scare him, not hit him."

That was a relief, sort of. Part of Hunter welcomed the idea of King being hurt or chased away.

"Listen, the boy is telling the men they have to leave the colony, that they have to go. He's threatening them somehow," the raccoon said. "They are afraid of him."

Hunter could see it in their tense bodies. All animals reacted the same way when they were afraid. They lower their heads and back away.

"Is he going to attack them?" Hunter asked.

"He might. They are afraid of that and, strange, did you just hear what the boy said? I can't believe what I'm hearing. He just called King by his name. He called him King."

"I didn't hear that," said Hunter.

"He called him King. He said he was the king of the colony. How did he know that?" the raccoon asked.

"Maybe he knows the biggest cat is always king."

"Perhaps, but that wouldn't explain the other thing he said." The raccoon paused and looked directly into Hunter's eyes. "He mentioned you. He called you Hunter."

"What?"

"He knows your name."

"That's impossible," Hunter said. "Are you sure?"

"I am sure. He said you and King were the leaders of the colony."

"I'm not a leader," Hunter protested.

"Yes, you are," the raccoon said. "There is no point in arguing. The real question is how does this boy know both your names?"

"Maybe he understands some of our language," Hunter said.

"I don't think humans can understand animals. Maybe he can sense your names. Maybe he has special powers. That would explain why the other humans are so afraid of him."

Hunter didn't have any explanation. He wished the colony cats were more cautious. Some of them had already started coming out of hiding and were creeping into the opening, drawn by the smell of the food. Would the boy chase them away again?

The boy seemed too occupied by the other humans to notice the cats. He and his mother were talking to them. While their words had become quieter, there was no indication that the boy was backing away.

"He wants them all to leave," the raccoon said.

"Do you think he can chase them away?" Hunter asked. "Is he strong enough? Does he have enough power?"

Before the raccoon could answer, the three started to walk away, along with the boy and his mother. He was making them go. This boy *was* powerful, a powerful friend to the colony.

Fifteen

Hunter could smell the boy before he could see him. Humans looked similar, but they had different odors. From the footfalls, he could tell the boy was alone. Often he came to the junkyard with some other boys and a girl. But whether by himself or with others, he always brought food.

The weather had changed from cool to cold. Hunter climbed up to his favorite place. It was high above the ground, protected from the wind but not the sun, which warmed the metal of the wrecks. From there he could survey the whole colony, but he was also high enough not to be bothered by King. The tension between King and Hunter was growing. Soon the two of them wouldn't be able to ignore it. Hunter hoped a fight wouldn't come anytime soon. Time worked in his favor. Each day that passed, King got older and Hunter got bigger, stronger.

Humans weren't much different from other animals. They didn't look down, and they certainly didn't look up. He was safe.

The boy entered the clearing slowly. He never moved quickly. There was a certain fluidity to his movements. Hunter knew it was impossible, but the boy moved like a cat, a two-legged human cat.

Some of the other cats watched as the boy entered the clearing. Others came out of hiding to greet him and eat the food he brought. King stood off to the side. He still hadn't forgiven the boy for tossing the rock at him, even though Hunter had explained to King and the colony that the boy had been protecting them. But the boy had food. In King's mind, that was reason enough to forget, even if he didn't forgive.

Hunter looked around for Mittens and the kittens. Mittens was nowhere to be seen and only one of the kittens was playing nearby. None of them were kittens anymore. They were teenage cats and often roamed the neighborhood on their own.

Hunter had taken them out hunting a few times. He had thought it would be a bother to have them along, and at first he was right. They were far too bouncy and impatient to do anything except scare away any prey he hoped to catch. But he was a good teacher. They all respected him, and he enjoyed showing them the skills they would soon need. In the last few weeks the kittens had finally caught on, and the proof was soon in their mouths and in their stomachs. Three out of the four of them had killed mice, and the fourth had managed to bring down a rat almost half his size. Hunter was learning new things too. He felt lucky that he had his mentor, the raccoon, to help guide him. He wanted to be that for his kittens. Maybe they could grow from a group of two—he and Mittens—to a group of six. Maybe, just maybe, cats could learn to live *together* and not just with each other.

Hunter was also learning to trust the boy. But Mittens went too far sometimes. One day, she had gone right up to the boy and rubbed against his leg. She had risen up on her back legs, so he could pet her, and scratch behind her ear.

Hunter had watched them in silence. He had been so afraid for her, so helpless to do anything, and then a strange feeling grew in him. Jealousy. It wasn't jealousy of the boy petting Mittens. He was jealous that she was being pet. He knew how her little girl liked to pet her. He wondered what it felt like. Would he ever be brave enough to allow the boy to scratch him behind his ear?

He watched the boy. As always, he moved slowly and deliberately. He was quiet and his face was still. If Hunter were ever to allow a human to scratch him, it would be—

Hunter tensed. Footfalls approached and they were coming fast!

Hunter got to his feet as two dogs raced into the clearing. They hesitated for a second at the sight of the boy and then charged forward. The dogs were so close together it was like they were a large eight-legged creature. They brushed by the boy and ran toward the cats. Cats and kittens scrambled, rushing for shelter as the dogs tried to chase all of them at once. One of the dogs grabbed a kitten and tossed it into the air. The kitten landed heavily and rolled and rolled, then stumbled to its feet and tried to get away. The dogs closed in on it before it could escape. Hunter, a black blur, jumped down and landed on the back of the bigger dog.

The dog howled in pain and surprise as Hunter tightened his grip and rode the dog like it was a horse and he was a cowboy. The dog twisted and turned, trying to shake Hunter loose. He reached his head back to try and grab Hunter with his teeth.

"Take that!" Hunter hissed as he struck the dog, clawing its delicate muzzle. The dog screamed, and its legs buckled, sending it to the ground. Hunter flew through the air and landed heavily against a car. Hunter gasped.

When he stumbled to his feet, pain shot through his right paw. He tried to get away, but the second dog was in front of him snarling, snapping and growling. Hunter turned to face him. He puffed himself up, hissed and snarled back. He had to fight the urge to turn and run.

"Go away or you'll get the same as the first dog!" Hunter yelled. The dog knew enough not to challenge Hunter's claws. He stopped advancing and froze.

"Maybe you're not as stupid as you look!" Hunter said. It was best to be bold when threatened. He didn't want the dog to sense his fear—or know the pain he was feeling.

Then the second dog, blood dripping down its side, joined the first dog. Together they inched forward.

Without looking back, not daring to turn his head, Hunter knew there was nothing but metal behind him. There was no way to jump onto it or over it. He was cornered. If he bolted to the left or right across the clearing, the dogs would grab him from behind.

For the first time, Hunter was afraid. The dogs were much bigger than him, and he was outnumbered.

There were so many cats living in the colony. If only a few got together to attack, they could easily drive the dogs away. But he knew that wouldn't happen. They were cats, and he was a cat. This was his battle alone to fight.

The boy screamed so loud Hunter jumped and the dogs turned their heads. The boy reached down, picked up a rock and threw it at the dogs. It landed off to the side, bouncing past them to hit one of the wrecks.

The smaller of the two dogs spun around, away from Hunter and toward the boy. It growled and bared its teeth at the boy. It looked like it was going to attack the boy. Hunter was shocked. What was that dog doing? Dogs didn't attack humans, they obeyed them. But maybe not all of them. Maybe these two were tired of leashes and orders. Hunter knew if somebody kept him on a leash, he would attack them.

With the one dog looking away and the second one distracted, Hunter had an opportunity to flee. He could dash under a wreck. But what about the boy? If Hunter ran off, what would happen to the boy? He was a human—he couldn't run very fast and he couldn't climb any better than the dogs could.

Hunter was in danger because he had rushed to defend a kitten—a kitten that wasn't even *his*. Cats didn't do that. And now he was going to do something even less catlike. He wasn't going to abandon the human. He was going to stay and fight the dogs. If the boy could rush in to save Hunter, Hunter couldn't leave the boy to fight alone. Hunter took a step toward the dogs. He hissed loudly to get their attention.

The boy yelled, and the dogs looked back at the boy. The boy reached over and grabbed two pieces of metal— one long and the other round and shiny. He slammed the long piece against the ground and the dogs jumped. They were still growling, but Hunter heard there was a difference in the tone. They were afraid and growling in *defense,* not *offense.* The boy slammed the two pieces of metal together with a crash and charged forward. The dogs yelped and ran away.

The boy dropped the metal pieces to the ground and bent over. Hunter looked at the boy and the boy looked up at him. Hunter nodded his head ever so slightly and the boy did the same. Then Hunter limped back to his den, unable to place any weight on one of his front paws.

Sixteen

"Is it any better today?" Mittens asked.

"A little better," Hunter said. That was a lie.

Mittens wasn't convinced, but she knew better than to question him further. He had been in the den for three nights and three days. He had only left for a couple of brief trips above ground. It had been three days since he'd had anything more than the tidbits of food Mittens had brought down into the den for him. Unable to hunt, barely able to walk, he hadn't been able to gather food for himself, or for her and their kittens. If it hadn't been for the boy and the others bringing food, they would have starved. Every night the kittens attempted to hunt, but without Hunter to guide them, they'd come back with nothing.

"It was very brave what you did," she said.

"It was very stupid!" he snapped.

"Those dogs would have killed that kitten if you hadn't acted."

"And instead they…" He stopped himself. He almost said they had killed him instead. But he didn't want Mittens or the kittens to hear. If he couldn't hunt, how would they survive? He knew his foot wasn't healing. It was getting more painful by the day.

"If I had been there, I would have helped," she said.

"Then there would have been two of us hurt," he said.

"But thanks to you, nobody died."

Not yet, he thought, not yet.

"I'm going to go out hunting with the kittens," she said.

"It's dangerous," he said.

"We'll be careful. You've taught the kittens well. You've taught us all well. Why don't you come up and see us off."

"I'm going to stay in the den," he said.

"No, you're not. You need to get out."

"I'm better to stay—"

"No!" she snapped. "This is *my* den and you're going to go out, right now!"

And it was her den. She was the mother.

Hunter could have argued with her, but he didn't. "Whatever you say."

He followed her up the incline of the tunnel to the surface. Each step sent a bolt of pain through his paw.

"Now, isn't that better?" she said.

"Much," he said. He sat down, the paw touching the ground but bearing no weight.

The kittens, their kittens, all gathered around.

"I need you all to be careful," he said.

"Yes, Father," one said, and the rest of them nodded in agreement.

"Work together. Remember to watch out for each other."

"We will," another replied.

"Be careful of cars, humans and dogs, especially dogs."

They nodded solemnly in agreement. They were good kittens.

"Wish us luck," Mittens said.

"Good luck," he said. But he thought they would need more than luck.

They left, leaving Hunter behind. But he wasn't alone. Other cats in the colony were nearby and watched him. He knew what they were thinking. He had heard bits of conversations and overheard the questions. The colony was completely divided. Some, mainly the females and especially the mothers, saw him as a hero. Others thought him a fool to have rescued the kitten and that he should have minded his own business.

Mittens hadn't been in the wild long enough to know what would happen next. And Hunter hadn't told her. If she had overheard the talk, she pretended she hadn't. The cats who had been feral for a long time all knew a cat that had died of an infection. If Hunter's paw didn't get better soon, he would be in trouble. If this was his end, he could accept it. What choice did he have?

What he couldn't accept was what would happen to Mittens and their offspring. Who would look after them?

Maybe he had been foolish to fight the dogs. But he had had to do it. It was the right thing. His injury was proof of it. Dogs working together had done this to him. Cats not working together had allowed it to happen. His death would be a symbol to those who thought he was a fool to intervene, a testament to what he now knew and believed. He wished the raccoon was there to talk to.

"Excuse me."

He startled out of his thoughts. It was a she-cat, the mother of the kitten he'd saved.

"I'm sorry to bother you."

"It's no bother. How is your kitten?" Hunter asked.

"He's up and running like nothing had happened. I just wanted to thank you," she said.

"You already did thank me."

"I wanted to thank you again." She paused. He knew there was more she wanted to say. He could see it in her eyes. "I want you to know I won't forget what you did, and neither will my kittens."

"That's nice to hear."

"I'm not much of a hunter," she continued. "Not like you, but no matter what happens, I am here for Mittens. I'll help her."

"I appreciate that."

He knew she was saying that if he died, she'd help out.

"I think cats should work together," she said. "If we all treated each other well, we wouldn't have to fear dogs and maybe not even humans."

"Dogs for certain," Hunter said.

"I just want you to get better. Then when you become king—"

"Let's not say such things," Hunter said. He glanced around, looking for King. Thank goodness he was across the clearing, out of earshot. The last thing he needed was a confrontation with King.

"I appreciate your thoughts. Helping Mittens, helping any other cat in the colony, is a good thing, and I thank you. If you'll excuse me though, I think I want to take a nap."

"Of course."

Normally he would have climbed up the wrecks to take advantage of the afternoon sun and safely observe the ground below. He couldn't do that now. He couldn't jump or run. Those were Hunter's two advantages. If he ever had to fight King without his full mobility, he would be easy for King to finish off.

There were only a couple of places he was safe, if King decided to fight him. The den was one—the passageway down was too narrow for King—and the few small places underneath the wrecks he had discovered. He headed to one of them slowly, deliberately. His paw couldn't bear much weight, and he knew he was being watched. He didn't want the other cats to know how bad his infection was.

He reached a safe spot and slipped underneath a wreck. If it hadn't been so small he would have made this place into a den for Mittens and their kittens. It was a shame it wasn't a little bit bigger. But cats didn't dig their own dens. They lived in ones abandoned by other animals. And then he thought about it. Why couldn't cats dig their own dens? Cats had paws and claws.

If a skunk or a rabbit could dig, why couldn't a cat? But those were the kinds of thoughts that had already gotten him into trouble.

What Hunter didn't realize was he had no reason to fear King. King was not interested in a confrontation. He saw no point in fighting Hunter. To King, Hunter was already dead. By attacking Hunter, King could only expose himself to the danger of being injured.

King knew an injured cat was a desperate and dangerous cat. There was no question he could kill Hunter if he wanted. But there was the possibility of Hunter inflicting injury on him. A bite to the flank, a claw in the eye—either could be as fatal to King as the wound Hunter was suffering from. To fight Hunter was a danger. To sit and wait for him to die was safe.

King had heard the rumblings too. Not just about Hunter becoming king, but also about Hunter's wish for the cats to learn to work together. He thought it was ridiculous, doglike. The idea would die when Hunter did.

Hunter heard sounds and felt the vibrations in the ground. Humans were approaching. He started back up toward the surface as the sounds and vibrations grew stronger. They must have been just above his head. Hunter cowered in the darkest corner.

The rumbling stopped, but the voices continued. Whoever they were, they were right outside Hunter's hiding spot. Then he recognized one of the voices, and one of the smells. It was the boy, and he'd brought food. But who was with him?

Taking food from the boy was breaking his word to his mother. Besides, he still felt taking the food was like robbing it from the cats and kittens who couldn't hunt. He knew King didn't feel that way, but he did. Now that he couldn't hunt, he thought about accepting some of the food—his mother would understand. If only Mittens was here, she might bring him down something. Instead he'd have to go out if he wanted something.

The voices soon faded, but the smell of the food remained. There was food just outside the entrance where he was hiding. All he had to do was go up and get it. If he didn't, then some other cat would take it. He could tell they were no longer right above him.

Slowly he started up the incline. The smell of the food grew, drawing him out. His stomach was so empty, and he knew food would fuel his recovery. He stopped just before the surface. The food was still there, but the humans weren't. He peeked out and his eyes confirmed what his nose had told him.

But what was that thing? It wasn't there a few minutes ago. It was a metal box, and he could see through it, see the food inside. He tried to figure out what the box was. He'd never seen one before. It was like a small garbage can tipped on its side. They had brought it for him.

He limped out of the hole and toward the food. None of the other cats were in the clearing. The only food was inside the metal container. Was it dangerous? If he hadn't been injured, if he wasn't so hungry, he wouldn't have gone any closer, but he had to eat.

He edged forward, staying low to the ground, watching, listening, smelling. He could still smell the humans. He could see the food, but he couldn't get to it. And then he saw an opening. Carefully, reluctantly, Hunter leaned in to fish the food out with his good paw. But he wasn't able to support himself very well and almost tumbled forward. He'd have to get closer. He stepped partway in. He reached and again he came up short. He'd have to climb farther in.

He hesitated and looked around. He could just step in, take the food and get out. It would take no time. He placed his front legs inside and then his back legs. He reached out to grab the food and—

There was a loud explosion. The surface on which he stood bounced up into the air. He spun around and lunged forward, crashing into the side of the container.

He turned the other way and the same thing happened. He jumped but hit metal. The opening was gone!

The boy and a big human raced toward him. Hunter scrambled, smashing against the mesh, trying to escape, but he was trapped. Hunter looked at the man and then at the boy. He couldn't believe the boy was doing this. The boy was no different than all the other humans. Hunter locked eyes with the boy, glaring at him. Hunter wasn't just angry at the boy for tricking him, he was angry at himself for falling for it.

Hunter felt a sharp pain and jumped. The man was holding something in his hand—something he'd poked into Hunter. Hunter snarled and hissed and then his whole body went numb, his vision got blurry. What was happening to him? What was…?

Hunter opened his eyes. His vision was blurry. It was bright, and he couldn't make out much of anything. He was still inside the container. Before his eyes could focus, he heard dogs barking and cats crying in distress. He could smell the dogs and cats, but there were other smells present he couldn't identify.

He got to his feet and almost tumbled over. He was wobbly, hardly able to stand. Hunter looked down.

His injured foot was wrapped in cloth. His paw felt numb, dead. He remembered what Mittens had told him about having her claws taken away. He flexed his muscles, and tried to reveal his claws. He couldn't feel them, he couldn't see them. No, he could feel them on the one foot, the one not covered in cloth.

He smelled water and found a little puddle in the corner. His mouth was dry. He lapped up the water. It felt as if the liquid cleared his mind. He moved to the front of the cage and noticed that something was different with his paw. It didn't shoot out jabs of pain with each step, but something wasn't right.

Staying low, he looked around. He was in a cage, and there were more cages surrounding him. He could see animals inside the cages. Most of them were filled with dogs, all of whom seemed to be barking or howling or whining. Then he heard a cat not far away.

"Hello!" he called out.

Two cats answered. One he could see, and another one farther away.

"Where am I? What is this place?" he asked.

"You don't know?" the closer cat answered.

"If I knew, I wouldn't be asking," he snapped and then felt bad. He wasn't in a position to be short with anybody. "I don't know, but if you could help me I'd appreciate it."

The cats talking to each other excited the dogs. Their barking grew louder.

"This is the vet's den," the cat shouted.

"And what is a vet?" Hunter asked.

"You don't know what a vet is?" said the cat. "Haven't you ever been to the vet before?"

"Never," Hunter said. "I've never been here."

"That's hard to believe. You're not a kitten. Where does your owner usually bring you?"

"Owner? I don't know that word. What is an owner?" he asked.

"The human who cares for you," the cat said.

"No human cares for me."

"Then how did you get here?" the cat asked.

"I don't really know. I live on my own with my colony in the junkyard."

"That's where you *used* to live," the cat said. "You're here now. So, soon you will have an owner. Soon you'll be living in his den."

Hunter didn't know what to say. Is that what happened? Is that why he was here? Is that why the boy had acted like a friend, so that he could trick him, trap him and make him live inside like a *dog*?

He looked down at his white-clothed foot. He couldn't see through it, and he couldn't feel anything under it. Were his claws gone?

Seventeen

Hunter stared through the bars of the cage. He was relieved to see the boy and his mother, but that didn't stop him from trying to strike at them through the bars.

He surveyed his surroundings. He was inside a human den, the boy and his mother's den. Hunter had sat on enough window ledges to know what they looked like. But he never thought he would be trapped inside one. On the other side of the room he saw a window, but he wasn't close enough to see anything out of it except sky. A few pigeons would sit on the ledge for a couple of minutes and then fly away. More than ever he wished he could fly, but even a bird couldn't get out of this cage.

He got up and paced. For the thousandth time that day he circled the cage, looking for an opening, a way out. There *had* to be an opening somewhere. He had stepped through it to get into the cage, so it existed. He just had to wait for it to open again. When it did, he'd be ready.

It had taken a full day before he realized he still had all his claws. By the second day, the swelling in his paw was gone and he could put his full weight on it. When the boy entered the room on day three, he had almost forgotten it was wounded.

Hunter glared at the boy, and then he softened his eyes. For the first few days, Hunter was furious with the boy. He had tricked Hunter, trapped him and kept him in a cage.

Hunter had learned the boy's name was Taylor because he reacted whenever his mother said that word.

Taylor spent a lot of time with Hunter. He sat by the cage, talking softly and gently offering food, first through the little slot in the side of the cage, and then finally he just pushed little pieces through the bars. At first, Hunter had refused to take the food. If Taylor knew Hunter was a hunter, then why did he keep him in that little cage, unable to hunt, unable to move? If he stayed in the cage, he was going to starve. It was better to die than live in a cage. The food smelled good.

He needed to eat if he wanted to live. He had no choice. Besides, Taylor had never given the cats bad food. If he wanted Hunter dead, he could easily kill him.

Hunter's foot got stronger over time. Taylor spent hours sitting with him. When Hunter looked into Taylor's eyes one day, he finally saw what Mittens had. Taylor was not there to hurt him. Somehow being trapped and caged had something to do with Taylor trying to help him. Hunter had one question—how long would he have to remain here?

From across the room, Hunter could tell Taylor had brought food, chicken. Hunter had never eaten it, but he recognized the smell. Taylor held out a piece, and Hunter cried out. He wanted the chicken. Hunter pricked his ears up to listen. Sometimes Taylor said things. Of course Hunter could not understand much of what he had said, but he had learned a few words. Taylor had mentioned King and Mittens before. Hunter couldn't help but worry about Mittens. It was a worry he couldn't do anything about. And then Taylor said *junkyard*. Taylor leaned close and pushed the piece of chicken through the bars. Hunter gently took the piece of chicken from his fingers.

Taylor put his face against the bars. Hunter was hesitant, but then he eventually moved toward the bars. Taylor pulled out another piece of chicken, and Hunter took it. Hunter couldn't believe how good the chicken tasted, or that he was allowing Taylor to feed him.

Taylor continued to talk. He said something about *home*. Hunter wasn't sure if he had said he was going to take him home, or explaining why he had taken Hunter away from his home. Hunter looked deep into Taylor's eyes. Taylor was friendly, gentle. His eyes didn't lie.

Hunter rubbed against the inside of the cage. Taylor pressed his hand against the bars and scratched Hunter behind the ears. Hunter began to purr.

Eighteen

Hunter tried to stay on his feet as the cage bounced around the back of a moving car. This might be his second time in a car, but it was still as terrifying.

The noise and the stench of the car were overwhelming. He hoped the trip would end soon. He could feel the car slow down and come to a stop. Was this the end, or would it start moving again like it had so many times before? Then there was silence. Not complete silence. He could still hear noises in the background. But the car was silent and still, and the vibrations had stopped.

Taylor, his mother and a man—the vet—talked. There were metallic clanging sounds and then a loud slam. Hunter jumped. The car door opened, letting in light, and Taylor was standing beside him. He reached in and picked up the cage. Hunter crouched and tried to stay balanced.

Hunter soon realized where he was. They were in the alley beside the junkyard. Hunter's heart raced. He was home...well, almost home. If only he wasn't in the cage.

Hunter cried out, meowing, "I'm here! I'm here! Mittens, can you hear me?"

There was no answer, but he hadn't expected one. The vet pulled back the junkyard fence to make a hole wide enough for them all to fit through. They were in the junkyard! Hunter was so excited he called out again. His meow was so loud Taylor almost lost his grip on the cage.

As they approached the colony, the humans talked. Hunter should have been listening, but he was too excited. They were getting closer and closer to the colony.

As they approached the clearing, Taylor walked ahead and the other two humans fell behind. There were cats in the clearing. A couple of them roused from slumber, and one got to his feet. They hadn't noticed Hunter was in the cage, or had they? A few cats poked their heads out of the wrecks and others entered the clearing. Why weren't Mittens or the kittens here? Was something wrong, had something happened to them? He had to get out of the cage. He had to go find them.

"Mittens, I'm back!" he yelled. His tail swished back and forth anxiously. He had to get out!

Taylor put the cage down. He rattled something and an opening appeared in the side of the cage. Hunter tensed. He had a way out. All he had to do was jump through the opening before it closed again. But he was too confused to move. He owed Taylor something. How could he say thank you? Hunter pressed against the bars, touched Taylor's hand and started to purr. Taylor pet Hunter's head through the bars. It felt good, but this wasn't his life.

Hunter sprung through the opening and landed a few lengths away. He should have run, but he didn't. He spun around and looked Taylor right in the eyes.

Taylor smiled. Hunter nodded, turned and walked away, toward the other cats. They looked shocked to see him. It was as if he had returned from the dead. None of them had expected to see him again. But these weren't the cats he wanted to see. If only—

"Hunter!"

"Daddy!"

Mittens and their four kittens raced up and practically bowled him over. "I thought—I thought I'd never see you again," Mittens said.

"Did you think you could get rid of me that easily?" he asked.

Mittens pushed her face against his. "I never wanted to get rid of you."

"Let's go home," Hunter said.

Hunter started toward the den. He was here, with his mate and his family. He was almost home. He was so happy. And then, out of the corner of his eye, he saw something move and he jumped. A blur rushed by him. King! Hunter spun around, puffed out his fur and snarled.

"I'm going to rip you apart!" King hissed as he took a swipe at Hunter.

Hunter dodged his blow and leaped onto the roof of a car. He crouched down, ready to strike if King followed, but he didn't.

"You're going to regret ever coming back here!" King screeched.

"So far you're the only one who seems to be bothered about it."

"Come down here, and I'll show you," King said.

"Why don't you come up here, and I'll show you, unless of course you're too fat to jump this high."

They both knew it would be to Hunter's advantage if King tried to jump.

"No need for me to go up there," King said. "Eventually you'll have to come down and—"

"Leave him alone!" Mittens screamed.

"Stay out of this," King said.

"Leave her alone!" Hunter said.

"Or what?" King asked.

"Or else you'll be the one who's ripped to shreds."

"You think you can do that?" King asked.

Taylor rushed forward, shouting. He threw a rock at King and it bounced off the ground beside him.

"Not me. I'll have help, and it won't be from other cats," Hunter said.

King looked shocked.

"You bother me, my mate or my kittens and that human will hurt you," Hunter said. "He does what I tell him to do."

"Do you really think I believe that?" King asked.

"Let's find out." Hunter turned to face Taylor. "It's all right. You can leave him alone." He paused. "For now."

King looked up at Hunter, and Hunter could see his doubt. But more than doubt, he saw fear.

Nineteen

"What do you make of it?" Hunter asked.

"I'm not sure," the raccoon said. "Humans are difficult to understand, even for me."

They were staring at the newly erected fences that surrounded the junkyard. Working from first light until just before sunset, a group of humans with loud machines had torn down the old metal fence and put up a higher, more solid wooden fence around the whole yard.

"Do you think it is a good thing or a bad thing?" Hunter asked.

"It could be a good thing *and* a bad thing."

"How could it be both?"

"It's much more solid. There are no holes for dogs to get in."

"That's a very good thing," Hunter said.

"But cats and the humans who feed you also use those same holes," the raccoon said.

"And humans who might want to hurt us."

"It sounds like you're making my point—good and bad," the raccoon said.

"I guess you might be right. But still, why would they change the fence around the junkyard?"

"Humans are hard to understand," the raccoon said. "Maybe I should be asking you about them."

"Why me?"

"I'm not the one who has been inside a car twice or had humans fix me when I'm injured. I'm not the one who tells humans what to do."

Hunter moved in closer. "You know I can't *really* do that, right? They don't really do what I ask."

"I know. The important thing is, how long do you think you can keep King convinced that you can?"

"I don't know, but every day I do is a good day. I have him confused and worried."

"You have all of us confused. Which is why I think I should ask you about humans," the raccoon said. "Perhaps the student has become the teacher."

"No," Hunter said. "I'm not the teacher. I've learned so much from you or by watching humans and rats and even dogs. There's so much to learn from animals."

"And there's so much the other cats could learn from you. You are going to be a very wise leader of the colony."

"If King doesn't rip me to shreds first."

"Just so you know, if he ever harms you, he won't live long enough to gloat," the raccoon said.

Hunter gave him a questioning look.

"I still believe in goodwill and peace, but I can make one little exception. I'll make sure it's quick. Who knows, he might even come back as a higher life form," said the raccoon.

"He has nowhere to go but up," Hunter said. "But right now, I'm more worried about the new fence than I am about King." He paused. "Should I be worried?"

"It's hard to tell with humans. My guess is that the fence has nothing to do with the colony."

"So we don't have to worry."

"Not necessarily. You have to understand, most of the time the humans don't do anything deliberately to hurt us."

"That's good to know."

"But remember, when a car runs over a cat, even though it's not deliberate, the cat is still dead.

Either way, I think you need to climb over to the other side of this fence."

The raccoon scrambled up the fence, digging in his sharp claws, dropped over the side and disappeared. Hunter leaped up to the top of the fence.

"Why is one side different from the other?" he asked as he perched on the top.

"Because of what is on the outside of the fence. Come and look."

Hunter jumped down. The outside of the fence was different. There were images on it—images of tall human dens.

"I've seen posters like that before. There's one at the front gate where the man with the cloth on his head stays," Hunter said.

"That poster is gone. These new ones are on all the fences, all the way around the junkyard."

"Why do they do that, put pictures all over?" Hunter asked.

"Sometimes it means nothing," the raccoon said.

"And other times?"

"Other times it means that what is in the picture will become real."

"The junkyard could become…become…like that?"

"I don't know. It could."

"But there were pictures of their dens there before and nothing has ever happened," Hunter said.

"Something did happen. The humans put up these new fences and new posters. They seldom do this much work unless it means something."

Hunter looked up at the poster and then looked away. He couldn't think about any of this right now. He already had too much on his mind.

Twenty

"Keep silent and stay with me," Hunter said.

His four teenage kittens fell in line behind him as he traced a path through the wrecks. It was important that they stayed with him now, but it didn't matter how loud they were. They wouldn't be heard over the sounds that filled the junkyard. The constant drone of engines, the stink of fumes and frequent crashing noises filled the air and caused even the calmest cat to jump. Hunter worked hard not to react. He needed to set an example for his offspring. He had become better at staying calm during the past three days that it had been happening. But still, some crashes were louder than others.

Mittens was having a lot of trouble, maybe more than any other cat in the colony. She was a house cat and jittery to begin with. The noises had upset her so much that she spent most of her time in the den and hardly ever came out at all.

This was the first time that cars had driven in the junkyard in the entire time Hunter had lived with the colony. The older cats in the colony remembered when that used to happen. They tried to offer reassurances to everybody. It had happened before and it had stopped. And even if it didn't stop, the cats would still be able to live there. The colony wasn't worried. But Hunter was, even if he didn't show it.

King was close at hand, always, and Hunter was sure he was only waiting for an opportunity to pounce. The only things keeping Hunter safe were his cautious nature and King's fear that Hunter could make Taylor do what he wanted. It didn't hurt that the raccoon was coming to visit Hunter either. The raccoon never talked to King, just gave him an evil glance. King was concerned that if Hunter had made friends with humans and raccoons, who else had he befriended?

Hunter was the talk of the colony. The cats were amazed at his tales—the car rides, the human den, his return to the colony. Of course, while there were many who thought well of him, there were others, besides King, who didn't. Some of the older cats, particularly the toms, didn't approve of his relationship with Mittens and their kittens. It wasn't natural for a tom to be so attentive to his family. And why did he take his teenage kittens with him everywhere and talk about cats working as a group? That was dog talk. Was he going to make friends with dogs as well as humans and raccoons?

"Be more careful now," Hunter said.

His teenage kittens stopped at the edge of the last row of wrecks. Beyond them was an open patch of red crushed brick where the wrecks had been taken away. Cars and humans filled the yard. The humans yelled and piled wrecks on top of trucks to be shipped away. The only thing more overwhelming than the noise was the smell. Big trucks belched out fumes and blue smoke rose into the air.

The humans were working where the rat colony had been. As the wrecks were removed, the rats fled and became easy pickings for the cats. Hunter and his kittens had feasted on them. He always looked for the king rat, but he hadn't caught sight of him. He had either died or taken flight. Hunter wondered if a car could even harm the king rat's tough old hide. But he was sure the rat had simply left to set up a new colony somewhere else. Rats were survivors, and that rat was the king of surviving. Maybe Hunter, Mittens and their kittens should leave the junkyard as well. Hunter had found this colony after his old one was destroyed. Maybe he could find another one for them. He knew this area better than anybody in the colony. He traveled the longest and farthest from the colony to hunt. But Hunter knew there were no other colonies in the area, and no place near where he thought they could start one. He would have to travel farther away.

Hunter was surprised by how much more open the junkyard was now. Little by little, wreck by wreck, the rat colony's homes had been dismantled and taken away until there was almost nothing left. Hunter wouldn't have believed it was possible. The older cats said nothing serious would happen to the colony. But Hunter knew the humans and their cars could do *anything*.

Most of the cats didn't even realize what was happening. They knew men and machines were in the yard, but they stayed as far away as possible. Some of the cats didn't even want to hear what Hunter had to say. They did what they felt was right for themselves. They stayed close to home, remaining still and silent.

Hunter was worried for the colony, but there was no point in saying anything about it, at least not yet. He certainly couldn't talk to Mittens. She was already too nervous and didn't seem herself.

The only creature he could confide in was the raccoon, and even the raccoon didn't seem to know much. Regardless, Hunter needed to speak to him. Hunter would have to leave the yard to find him. But first things first. He saw a rat scurry past. Maybe dinner was served.

"Father," one of the kittens said.

"I see it."

Without saying another word, his children spread out, two in one direction and two in the other, so the rat would have no escape. He couldn't help but wonder, did the cat colony have a way to escape if it needed to?

Twenty-One

Hunter walked along the top of the fence. He could see in both directions—into the yard and into the neighborhood. The neighborhood looked as it always did, but the yard continued to change, day by day. It was still early. The yard was quiet. The men and machines hadn't arrived yet. He knew they would soon. Each day there were fewer wrecks and more open space. There was nothing left of the place where the rats had lived. Nobody would grieve for the rats. And so far, the area around the cat colony had been left untouched.

Somebody was coming down the alley. Hunter picked up the scent. It was the boy, Taylor. He was alone, but Hunter could tell he brought food. Hunter stood and waited as Taylor continued toward him, unaware of the cat's presence. If he sat still, Taylor wouldn't even notice him.

But Taylor *did* notice Hunter. Taylor looked up and smiled, then walked over and stood beneath Hunter. The cat lifted up a paw. He had seen the way humans greeted each other. Taylor smiled. His eyes were soft and friendly. Hunter put down the first paw and held up his other one. Taylor seemed to be even more pleased.

Taylor opened up the bag he was carrying, and the smell of the food drifted up to Hunter. He was hoping for chicken. It wasn't chicken, but it did smell good. Taylor took a piece of food and reached up to Hunter. The fence was so high Hunter had to bend down to reach it. It was good, some sort of meat. Hunter had never tasted it before, but he liked it.

Taylor said a few more words, which Hunter didn't hear very well, although he knew Taylor was going into the yard. With the new fence in place, there was only one way in—through the gate where the man with the cloth on his head stayed. Hunter knew Taylor would probably give him a few more tidbits, but there were other cats in the colony that needed it.

Hunter jumped down from the fence and into the yard. Through the fence he heard Taylor moving along the alley, heading toward that gate. Hunter could have crossed the yard and reached the colony before Taylor, but he needed to find the raccoon first. When Taylor had gone, Hunter jumped back up onto the top of the fence and leaped down into the alley.

Twenty-Two

The raccoon pulled out some food from the garbage can and offered it to Hunter.

"Thank you," Hunter said. It wasn't nearly as tasty as the meat Taylor had given him, but it was still good. Besides, Hunter wasn't here for food. He was here for conversation.

"How is your family?" the raccoon asked.

"The kittens are getting bigger all the time. They are becoming such good hunters," he said proudly.

"And Mittens?"

"She's…well, everything that's going on with the junkyard is upsetting her."

"It should be upsetting to everybody."

"Not everybody," Hunter said. "Some of the cats are acting like nothing is happening."

"They would have to be deaf and blind and without a sense of smell to not know something was happening."

"They know something is happening. They just don't believe it is going to affect them in a bad way." He paused. "Maybe they're right. What do you think?"

"What I think isn't important. What do *you* think?" the raccoon asked.

"I'm not sure what to think," Hunter said.

"Then what do you see? What is happening?"

"They're moving the wrecks out of the yard, but the older cats say that has happened in the past," Hunter said.

"I'm older than any of the cats in the colony, so I, too, remember that they used to move cars out of the yard all the time."

"So they're right?"

"They're *half* right," the raccoon said.

"How can they be half right?"

"Because they are half *wrong*."

"I don't understand," Hunter said. "Can you explain, please?"

"Certainly. When the junkyard was open, the humans moved the wrecks out."

"Like now."

"But they also moved cars *in*. Are they bringing any wrecks in or only removing them?"

"I'm not sure. They *could* be moving wrecks in."

"They could be doing anything, but don't tell me what you *want* to believe. Tell me what you *do* believe," the raccoon said.

Hunter thought about the increasingly large tracts of open space in the junkyard. He thought about the whole rat colony being gone. He thought about the cars he had seen leaving and how he had not seen any entering. He knew he had to think with his head, not his heart. He had to decide what *was* right, not what he *wanted* to be right.

"They're not moving wrecks in," he said. "They aren't filling up the yard, they are emptying it."

The raccoon nodded his head.

"But there are so many wrecks. The humans could get tired or give up before they get to our colony."

This time the raccoon shook his head. "These humans do not get tired or give up. They are going to clear out the entire yard, and that will be just the beginning. They will work until they have built new dens, tall dens. The dens will look like the pictures on the fence."

"How can you be so certain?" Hunter asked.

"Aren't you certain?"

Hunter was afraid to say what he believed. But not saying it wouldn't change it from happening. "I know we have to leave," he said. "I just don't know where we're going to go. Do you know a place?"

"I can look. I can ask other raccoons," he said. "Would it be a place for a few cats or for everybody?"

"Most of them won't be willing to leave."

"Then you need to convince them," the raccoon said.

"I don't know if I can."

"You have to. If they don't leave, they will die. Try to convince them. Who knows, they might realize you're going to be a good leader and leave with you."

Twenty-Three

Cats didn't have meetings. Any attempt to get them to attend a meeting would only result in fewer cats coming than would have been there by accident. Their meetings had to simply happen.

Hunter knew humans had meetings. He saw them every morning in the junkyard, standing together, talking and gesturing with their hands. They discussed what they were going to do next. Right after the meeting they would hurry off and dismantle another part of the yard.

There was no need for them to be sly or stalk the wrecks. The humans just attacked them like a pack of dogs. Maybe dogs had meetings too?

Hunter was tired of how independent cats were. Being independent left them divided. And being divided would lead them to be destroyed. Besides, how independent was the colony if it sat around waiting for Taylor and his pack to feed them? The colony was nothing more than a pack of dogs. The only difference was that they weren't wearing leashes or drooling, and they didn't stink.

Hunter looked around the circle of wrecks that ringed the clearing at the center of their colony. It was as if nothing had changed. Not one car had been removed. While the rest of the yard was exposed, this section remained unchanged. Maybe the colony would be spared after all. Hunter wondered if Taylor was controlling the humans and making them take other wrecks. He had seen him chase humans away before. Maybe Taylor wouldn't let them take these wrecks, and everything would be fine. But Hunter knew that was wishful thinking.

Hunter understood how the cats who didn't venture far from the colony could think nothing was wrong with what was happening to the junkyard. For them the human sounds and smells had always surrounded them. What existed now was the same, only stronger.

As Hunter entered the clearing, he counted the cats he could see. Twice he had counted every toe on every paw. There were other cats who remained out of sight. But when he spoke, they would be able to hear him. They might even come out, or they might wander away. There was no predicting.

His teenage kittens were with him, scattered around. They had already met as a family and discussed the need to leave the junkyard. They, of course, would do what their father wanted. They had explored the yard and knew that he was right.

Mittens was not with him. More and more she stayed in their den. Their den was the most protected place in the yard. Mittens was doing what most frightened cats would.

That instinct was Hunter's biggest challenge. He was going to have to convince a colony of cats that, first, they were in danger, and second, that since they were in danger they would have to leave. He couldn't even convince his mate to come out of the den, so what chance did he have of convincing all the other cats to leave? He knew Mittens would follow him and the kittens, but the others? Well, he had to try.

On the edge of the clearing, sitting on top of a car in a little halo of sunlight, sat King. He was watching Hunter, but also pretending to ignore him. Hunter did the same. That was their unspoken agreement— an agreement that was about to be broken. Hunter hoped that wasn't the only thing that was going to be broken. King could afford to look away from Hunter. Hunter was not going to attack him. Hunter would never have that luxury. He kept an eye on King. If the big cat caught Hunter by surprise, bowled him over or trapped him beneath his bulk, there would be no chance of escaping injury.

Hunter walked into the center of the clearing. He made sure not to face King. There was no point in waiting any longer. "We need to leave," Hunter shouted.

Several heads turned toward him. A few other cats turned their ears in his direction but looked away. Nobody responded.

"We need to leave the colony," he said louder. "It is no longer safe for us to be here."

"Yes, we need to leave," said another cat.

He looked over. It was his oldest male kitten. He had hoped it was another cat, but one voice was better than none. Two of his other kittens added their agreement.

"So now we know what Hunter and his kittens want," said King.

He turned to face Hunter, but he didn't get up. It was his way of saying Hunter and his ideas weren't worthy of rising to his feet for.

"It isn't safe here anymore," Hunter said.

"It looks safe to me," King replied.

"Then you're looking but not seeing," Hunter said.

He could see the hair on King's back rise.

"Or maybe you're seeing without thinking," King snapped. "It's sad that the *brave* Hunter is so afraid of a few loud noises and foreign smells."

"It's more than loud noises."

"Then you admit that you're afraid," King said.

"Of course I'm afraid," he said. "It is wise to be afraid when there's danger."

"The humans are just working in the yard," an old she-cat called out.

"There's nothing to worry about," said a second elder.

"They've done this before. You're just too young to remember," the old she-cat added.

"Not just too young, but too *new*," King said. "Some of us were born and raised in this colony. You were allowed to come and live here." He paused. "Perhaps I made a mistake by doing that."

"I'm more concerned about the mistake you're making in choosing not to leave," Hunter said.

"The mistake would be thinking there was danger when there isn't and leaving a perfectly good colony," King said. "A kitten jumps in fright and runs if a butterfly lands unexpectedly close."

"Those are awfully big butterflies fluttering around the junkyard taking away cars," Hunter said.

"Cars have *always* been taken away," an old tom said.

"Taken away and brought in," Hunter said. "Has anybody seen any cars being brought in?"

Nobody answered.

"Has anybody seen any cars taken away from this part of the yard?" King asked.

"None, not one," a cat behind Hunter said, and others voiced agreement.

There was no point arguing.

"Perhaps you've been spending too much time with that house-cat mate of yours. I've noticed she is too frightened to even come out of your den," King said. "Maybe you are afraid too?"

"Is there anybody here who questions my bravery?" Hunter asked. He looked around the clearing. Almost every cat was present. As Hunter looked at them, cat by cat, each one turned away or looked down at the ground. Nobody questioned Hunter's bravery, not even King.

"A good leader knows when to lead," Hunter said.

"And do you think you are a leader?" King asked. "Do you think you can be the king?" King slowly got to his feet.

"I think somebody has to be the leader," Hunter said.

"And you think that's you?" King snapped. "Is giving orders such as 'We all have to leave' going to be your legacy as the king? Do you think we are cats or dogs?"

"There are things we could learn from dogs," Hunter said and then realized he shouldn't have.

There were howls and cries and protests throughout the yard.

"Let him speak his mind," a she-cat shouted. It was the mother of the kitten he had saved. The noise died down. "When you make noise like that, you're acting like a pack of baying dogs. Let him speak."

Hunter wasn't sure what to say, but he knew he had to talk. "I know right now they haven't disturbed any of the cars around our colony, but it's only a matter of time."

"How can you be so certain?" another cat asked.

"I've studied humans, and I know them."

"Has one of them told you their plans?" another cat asked.

"I don't always understand them, but I understand their actions. They are going to clear away all the cars and build the dens pictured on the fences that surround us."

"I've seen no pictures," King spat.

"The pictures are on the other side of the fence. You haven't seen them because your life is only on this side," Hunter said.

"And your life may soon be on neither side of the fence!" King snapped. He jumped to the ground, and Hunter tensed, waiting for the charge, but it didn't come.

"You are free to leave at any time," King said. "In fact, I *invite* you to leave the colony, and take those runt kittens and house-cat mate of yours with you."

"My kittens are only half grown and already they're better hunters then you'll ever be," Hunter said. "And we will leave. But I don't want to leave the other colony cats behind to die when they could live."

"If there was danger, and there isn't," King said, "then the shortest route to death would be leaving. Do you have such little wisdom that you don't know a cat's den and familiar surroundings are the best place to be when there's danger?"

"What if those surroundings are the danger?" Hunter asked. "Wouldn't leaving be wise, instead of hunkering down in some hole?"

"If it's so dangerous, why don't you just tell the humans to leave us alone," King said. "Don't they listen to the wonderful Hunter?"

Hunter didn't answer. Of course they didn't, but he still needed King to believe he could tell them what to do, or at least Taylor.

"For all we know, maybe you're the one who has been telling them to remove the cars so we have to leave the junkyard!" King said.

"And why would I do that?" Hunter asked.

"So that you can be king," he snapped.

"I don't want to be the king," Hunter said. "I only want to be a good leader."

"Cats don't need leaders. Dogs need leaders. Besides, where exactly is it that you think we should go?" King asked.

"I don't have a place yet. The raccoon is looking for a good location where—"

"The raccoon!" King said. "First it was humans and now a raccoon! Should we wait to see what the rats and dogs think we should do too?"

"The rats have all left," Hunter said. "Their colony was removed and most of them killed. My *runt* kittens and I killed many of them. Even dogs run from danger. Are we not smarter than the dogs who know when danger is coming?"

"*Everything* is smarter than dogs except rocks and dirt. I am going to stay, but any cat who wishes to leave may leave. *That* is the way a real leader works. Just remember, any cat that leaves with Hunter is *not* welcome back. We will fill the colony with cats who wish to be cats, strong, independent, brave and wise cats."

"Shortly there will be no colony and no cats. To stay is to die," Hunter said. "My family will be leaving as soon as we've found another location. Any cats who wish to follow are welcome. Any cats that remain, I hope your death will be swift and without pain."

Hunter turned and walked away.

Twenty-Four

"How are you feeling?" Hunter asked Mittens. His voice was quiet and concerned.

"Okay. Tired, but okay. I thought it was supposed to be easier the second time," she said. "It was harder."

"I know, but you did well. I'm proud of you."

"Four seems to be the number."

"Four is a good number. Four kittens in our first litter and four kittens in our second," he said.

Hunter understood why she had been spending so much time in the den. If Mittens had been a more experienced parent, she would have known the kittens would be arriving. As it was, they were a surprise to both her and Hunter until close to the birth.

"And are they all fine?" she asked.

"How could they not be fine?" They were tucked under their mother, nursing, and difficult to tell apart.

"Their older brothers and sisters were asking when they can come down and see them," Hunter said.

"Not yet. Not for days. I'm too tired and they're too little."

"I'll keep them away then."

"Thank you." She paused. "Unless they need to come down to be safe. Is it safe up there?"

"Today is quiet. The yard is empty of humans."

"Even Taylor?" she asked.

"Taylor has not been here for three nights. None of them have," Hunter said.

"I'm sure he'll be back."

"I'm not so sure, and I don't know if it would be a good idea if he did," Hunter said. "As long as Taylor comes and feeds the cats, they won't want to leave the junkyard."

"How long do we have?" she asked. "Are they getting close to the colony?"

"Closer each day. It could be as many as ten days or as few as four. The humans are working quickly."

"Then you have to leave," she said.

Hunter laughed. "You know there's no way I would leave without you."

"And you know there's no way I can leave for at least ten days. The kittens are much too young to leave the den, let alone walk to a new colony."

"It isn't far. Well, not too far," Hunter said. "The raccoon has located a place. It isn't big, or as good as this one, but it will do. We could carry the kittens."

"No," she said, shaking her head. "You would have to carry me too. I can't go, not yet."

"You don't have to go yet."

"Is it a good place?" she asked.

"Better than here."

"Better than the junkyard now, or how it was before?"

He wanted to lie but he couldn't. "Better than what this will become. The new place is not perfect, but it's the best we could find."

"Have you convinced many other cats to join us?" Mittens asked.

"Not many. But I'll keep trying, and the raccoon will keep looking for other locations."

"Until then, maybe we should just stay—"

"We cannot stay here. We have to leave. We have no choice."

"You have a choice. You can leave, but I can't. You have to take the other kittens to safety."

"I'm going to take *all* my kittens to safety. And you."

He bent over and licked her head. She was the mother, but even a mother needed to be mothered sometimes.

There was a loud crash, and Mittens and Hunter jumped.

"I'll go and look," he said. "You're safe here. Just nurse the kittens. I'll be back."

Hunter sped up the tunnel, not even stopping before he exited. There was no time for caution.

All around him other cats had gathered to try and figure out what had happened. Even those who had been harboring the biggest doubts about a move were starting to rethink things. Some of them looked at Hunter, hoping he had an answer. He didn't, but he knew how to find one.

"Which way?" he asked.

Three or four cats gestured with their eyes. It was not the direction he had expected danger to come from, but he headed off that way.

He wanted to run ahead, but he was too wise. He took a route through narrow passages, which offered him some protection. It was the only path that gave him that opportunity. Almost the entire yard had been emptied. All that remained was a thin crust of cars surrounding the colony on one side and a few wrecks stacked between the colony and the fence in the direction he was heading.

He skidded to a stop. Where the fence should have been was a large, gaping hole. Part of the fence had been knocked down. How did that happen, and what did it mean? Were they going to start taking the wrecks away from that side of the yard instead? If they did, it wouldn't be good. That was the escape route Hunter had planned to use for the colony.

An engine started up. Out of nowhere a gigantic vehicle raced through the hole and crashed into the fence, knocking it over. Dust and dirt flew into the air. Hunter froze, too shocked and scared to move. A cloud of dust billowed up, and then there was silence.

Through the cloud of dust Hunter could see the man with the cloth on his head. He was on top of the big vehicle. Hunter had seen the vehicle pick up wrecks in other parts of the yard and take them away. The man was now going to start taking cars from this part of the yard too. A group of humans ran toward Hunter. Hunter saw Taylor. Taylor was here! They had knocked down the fence so the cats could escape.

Hunter looked at the other humans. He recognized Taylor's friends and Taylor's mother. Hunter remembered her from when he was injured and had stayed in their den. But there were others too. As many as all his toes. Some of them were strangers. Why were there so many of them? Had they all brought food? Food would be good. Hunter and his brood had been able to catch some food, more than the other cats had, but even he was still hungry.

Another vehicle pulled into the opening. Hunter recognized it instantly. It was the van he had been in. His body tingled. The sight brought back frightening memories. The van stopped and the vet climbed out. He opened the back door and pulled out a cage. And then another one, and another one, and another one. There were so many cages. Were there as many as there were cats in the colony? He couldn't even count that high. He had to go back and warn them.

Hunter needed to be quick. He started running and stopped. What was he going to say to the colony? What was Taylor doing? Why would he want to trap them all? Every time he thought he knew Taylor, the boy surprised him. Was Taylor good or bad? Did he really care for the cats? Maybe he was responsible for removing the wrecks, so the vet could trap the cats? Hunter had no answers. He had to tell the colony they were coming.

Hunter charged into the clearing with such speed he surprised several cats, who scurried away.

"What's wrong? What's wrong?" another cat demanded.

"The fence has been broken down…there are humans…lots of humans," said Hunter.

"Did they bring food?" the calico asked.

"I don't know if they have food, but they do have cages…lots of cages!" said Hunter.

Some of the cats knew what a cage was, but most of them didn't.

"Why would they have traps?" the old she-cat asked.

"I don't know, but I have to go to my den," Hunter said.

"Wait!" one of the cats called out.

"There's no time to wait!" Hunter yelled. "You all need to hide."

He ran to his den and slowed down at the entrance. He didn't want to rush in and frighten Mittens. A mother with new kittens could be easily spooked. Slowly, deliberately, he slipped into the den.

"Is everything all right?" Mittens asked.

He needed to answer truthfully but also not worry her. "It's all right in here. It's safe in here."

"And out there?"

"You're not going out there."

"But is it safe?" she asked.

"It hasn't been safe for a while. That's why we have to leave, when you're able."

They heard the humans enter the clearing.

"One of the humans is Taylor, and some of the others are his friends," Hunter said.

"Some of the others? How many are there?"

"Many. I should go and look."

"No," Mittens said. "I need you to stay here, to stay with me."

His curiosity was drawing him to the surface to look, but she needed him. He settled in beside her, the kittens between them, protected. But could he really protect them? Could he even protect himself?

The next few hours would tell. The sun had only just come up. He'd have to wait until dark, after the humans left, to leave the den and continue searching for a new place for his family. He sensed the movement of the kittens against his side. They were still so small. They needed more than a few hours.

Twenty-Five

Mittens startled when an angry cry echoed down the tunnel to their den. They had been bombarded with the loud noises of humans talking and walking across crushed rock all day. But the most disturbing sounds were the cries of the other cats. Hissing, snarling, plaintive meows, desperate moans, following the loud metallic snap of cage doors closing. Between all the clatter, Hunter slept. It was daytime, his time to sleep.

Hunter was tired. His sleep had been disturbed for days, his head filled with thoughts, worries, questions, concerns, wonders and decisions. When he was awake, he was often gone for long periods of time. Every day he searched for a new home, traveling farther and farther from the junkyard to look for a better potential home than the one the raccoon had found. It wasn't just the searching that was tiring, it was the *newness* of everything. There was so much to hear, smell, listen to, be aware of and try to understand. And he had to be cautious as he pushed through potentially dangerous situations.

Hunter was drained. But being a cat meant he was curious. Every time Hunter rose to leave the den, Mittens stopped him. She pleaded for him not to go. She wanted him to stay where they were safe. And they were safe, for now, but not for much longer.

Hunter felt divided between his broods of new kittens and the older ones. The older ones still needed his guidance, and the four new ones could not survive without him. Hunter knew what a mother cat could do if she became scared and protective of her newborns. He had heard tales of mothers killing their litters to save them from danger. But Mittens wouldn't do that, or would she? He couldn't take the chance, so he remained with her throughout the day. He kept her calm, offered reassurance and was there to stop her if she got desperate. The four older kittens stayed on the surface. They kept hidden during the day. They were cautious, observant and careful. But still, they weren't much more than kittens themselves. Finally, his concern for them took over.

"I'm going up to check," he said softly. "To make sure *all* our kittens are well."

"Be careful," she said.

"I will. It's getting quieter up there."

And it was. There seemed to be fewer human sounds. He was certain many of them had gone.

"Come back, soon, please," said Mittens.

"I won't be long."

He approached the surface slowly. He told himself to think, not feel. He stopped just short of the top and listened. There were scents and sounds of humans, but they were faint and far enough away they didn't pose a threat.

He poked his head out and looked around. No one was there. Everything looked familiar. For a split second, he thought everything had been part of an elaborate dream, but then he heard another clank. He resisted the urge to go back down the hole.

He darted out and found shelter under a wreck. What now? He knew he had to make his way to a spot where he could see the clearing. That's where the humans were.

Hunter knew the nooks and crannies of the wrecks well. He hoped his older kittens had stayed hidden in the wrecks too. He sensed another cat ahead in the narrow passage.

"I thought they had caught you," a big tom said.

"I'm not going to get caught," Hunter said.

"They've caught a lot of the cats. More than my toes and your toes together."

"Have you seen my kittens?" Hunter asked.

"I haven't seen them, but that doesn't mean much. I've been here most of the day."

"You're a wise cat," Hunter said.

"If I was really wise, I would have listened to you and we would all be gone by now."

"Staying in here is wise. They can't get you here," Hunter said.

"Not unless they remove the wrecks. Do you think they're going to do that?" the cat asked.

"Yes. Not today, but soon."

"Have you found a place for us to go?" the cat asked.

"There's a place. It's not as good and it's not close," Hunter said.

"There aren't that many left. When can we go?"

Hunter knew he couldn't go soon, but that didn't mean he couldn't lead some of the other cats there. "In a few days I can take you and anybody else who wants to go."

"Do we have a few days left?"

"I hope so, but I don't know. I have to go and find my kittens."

"Be careful," the cat said.

"I can stay away from the humans."

"They're not the only ones you have to fear. King said he is going to rip you apart, kill you."

Hunter shook his head sadly. "With all that we're facing, he still wants to come after me?"

"He blames you for all of this," the cat said.

"If he thought I had such powers that I could cause all of this, then he should be afraid that I'm going to kill *him* or *have* him killed."

"Maybe he is afraid. He's been hiding since this happened."

"Do you know where he's hiding?" Hunter asked.

"In the big pile of wrecks on the far side of the clearing."

That reassured Hunter. He could get to the clearing without having to pass by King. The last thing Hunter needed was to fight King. Especially in the narrow passages where Hunter's speed and agility would be hindered. The only place he had any chance against King was up in the clearing, and he certainly wasn't going out there.

There was a loud scream, a human scream, followed by the desperate cry of a cat. They were close, very close. Hunter froze in place. His every instinct was to turn and run away from the commotion.

But if he did that, he might as well have stayed inside the den.

Hunter started moving slowly forward. He wove his way past sharp edges and rusty parts. The cat and the humans were getting louder. He recognized the cat's voice. It was a tomcat he knew well. He sounded as if he was being throttled. And one of the human's voices was Taylor's.

Hunter approached the edge of the wrecks and peered out. The vet and Taylor were in the clearing. The vet held a long metal pole. The tomcat was attached to the end of the pole and he was being dragged forward. His claws dug into the crushed rock as he howled, and his eyes were wild with fear.

The vet pulled the cat closer. The cat swiped at him. But the vet pinned the cat to the ground. Taylor ran off and returned with a cage. He placed it on the ground and opened it. The vet grabbed the cat by the scruff of his neck, unfastened the pole and dropped him into the cage. The cat, free, lunged against the mesh, trying to find a way out.

The fur on Hunter's back rose up. He knew exactly what the cat was experiencing inside the cage. He knew the fear, helplessness and desperation of being trapped inside there. The vet picked up the cage, and he and Taylor walked away, disappearing from Hunter's view.

Hunter should have retreated, hidden. But he didn't. He scrambled across the clearing, following the vet and Taylor. They passed by some other humans but didn't stop. They headed toward the opening in the fence. It wasn't safe to follow directly behind them, but Hunter needed to know what they were going to do with the caged cat. He knew of another way to get to the opening, hopefully without being seen.

Hunter spun around and sprinted away. He hoped he didn't run into any other humans, and if he did, he hoped they wouldn't be fast enough to capture him. He stayed in the opening, close to the edge of the wrecks, so he'd have a place to run to if needed.

It was dusk, and Hunter felt the snow coming. He tolerated the snow but hated the cold. Tonight the temperature would drop. He wanted to go back and stay in his den, dry and warm. But he still needed to look for food and a new place for the colony.

He reached the fence. Wrecks were pushed up against it. One leap took him to the roof of a car, and a second brought him to the top of the fence. He jumped off, onto the ground on the other side. Now that he was outside the junkyard, the fence was his only defense from being seen. He ran along the base of the fence toward the place it had been knocked down and to where the van was parked.

As he approached, he heard the drone of cats—many, many cats—screaming and crying in desperation. He'd never heard such a…wait, yes he had. It was the sound of cats in cages, trapped. The colony cats were in cages.

He reached the gigantic gap in the fence, and up ahead was the van. The caged cats were inside. He could hear them. Then he saw the vet and Taylor. Hunter hid behind a large rock.

The vet and Taylor opened the back door of the van. There was an explosion of cat cries. The vet put the cage in the back and slammed the door shut. Now Hunter knew where all the cats had been taken. He just didn't know why.

Twenty-Six

It had taken most of the night to break the news to Mittens and comfort her. Their first litter couldn't be found. Either they had fled, were out hunting, or they had been captured and taken away. How could any of this be possible? Why was Taylor doing this? How could Hunter be so wrong about Taylor? And most important, where was Taylor taking the caged cats? Where were his kittens? He couldn't afford to spend any more time thinking about it. He had to care for Mittens and their newborn kittens.

"I have to go up," Hunter said.

"Do you have to?" she asked.

"Our kittens might be up there," he said. "They might be back by now. How are the little ones?"

"They're good, as good as they can be."

"Take care of them. I'll be back as soon as I can."

Once the humans had left, Hunter had gone hunting. He had gotten lucky and captured a rat that he had brought back to the den. It was enough for him and Mittens.

He left her behind and went up the tunnel. The ground was coated by a thin dusting of snow. It had washed away the scent of the humans, but it would take more than snow to remove what had happened.

He ambled into the clearing. There were no cats visible, but he knew they were hiding nearby.

"Help me!"

He turned. A young she-cat was trapped in a cage.

"Please, help me!" she called.

"Yes, and help me too!" another cat said. It was the blue cat, a tomcat Hunter liked. Hunter walked toward him.

"Can you open this?" the tom asked.

"I don't know how to open them."

"But you were in a cage and got out. How did you do that?" the blue cat asked.

"The human let me out. He pushed something and an opening appeared."

"Show me what he pushed."

Hunter shook his head. He wished he knew how to open the cage, but he didn't. "I just—" Human voices and footsteps approached.

"I'm sorry," Hunter said and ran off with the blue cat calling after him.

Hunter and a couple of cats who had crept into the open scrambled for cover. The only cats visible were the two in the traps.

There were fewer humans here now than before. The sound of their feet was weaker. Taylor, his mother, the other boy who was with him the most often, the vet and one other female human entered the clearing. Taylor was the leader even though he was not the biggest. They walked over to the two traps. Taylor picked up the one with the blue cat, and his friend picked up the one with the she-cat. They started back in the direction they came from.

Hunter slipped through the wrecks and emerged on the far side. He ran back to the fence, jumped on a wreck and leaped to the top of the fence, sliding on the dusting of snow before regaining his grip. From the fence he jumped into the alley. He wanted to know if these two cats were being loaded into the same van too. And more importantly, if it still contained the other cats and maybe his kittens. Was it possible his kittens were still out hunting?

The van was parked in the same place. But the two boys were nowhere to be seen. Hunter crept forward. He had wanted to get closer, find a spot to watch them from without being seen.

"Good morning, Hunter."

Hunter spun around, hissed and puffed out his fur.

"Usually you're the one who sneaks up on me," the raccoon said.

"I'm so glad to see you!" Hunter said. "There's so much happening that I don't understand."

"Like the fence being knocked over," the raccoon said.

"There's more…much more."

Hunter explained about the cages, the cats being taken away and how Taylor and the other humans were back taking more cats. Before he could finish, Taylor and the other boy emerged through the fence, carrying the two cats.

"That's the boy you trust," the raccoon said.

"That's Taylor, the boy I *did* trust."

They watched the back of the van open, and the sound of distressed cats rolled out into the alley.

"How many cats are in there?" the raccoon asked.

"Most of the colony, including my kittens, I think. I didn't expect Taylor to do something like this."

"You know what he is doing, but do you know *why* he is doing it?" the raccoon asked.

Hunter shook his head. "I wish I knew."

"Well, in that case, there's only one way to find out." The raccoon paused. "Let's go ask Taylor."

"What?"

"We'll just go over and ask him what he's doing."

"That's insane. I can't go over there. He'll trap me," Hunter said.

"You're right. You can't go. I'll go alone."

The raccoon started to walk away.

"No, you can't go either," Hunter said. "It's too dangerous."

"I want to listen to the boys. You would be amazed what you can learn if you listen. You go back to your den. I'll come find you later and tell you what I've learned."

The raccoon waddled down the alley. It didn't take long for the humans to notice him. The other boy yelled, pointed and took a step backward. Hunter crouched down, so they couldn't see him.

The raccoon stopped at the broken fence. He picked up a piece of it as if he was examining it. Hunter thought maybe the raccoon wasn't going to move any closer. He was brave—incredibly brave—and a true friend, but what good was it going to do? The raccoon started off toward the humans again, and Taylor slowly walked toward him. The raccoon sat down and Taylor continued to move forward. He sat down right in front of the raccoon. He was so close he could have grabbed the raccoon.

Hunter was stunned. What was going to happen next? But he didn't have time to stay and watch. He needed to get back to the den and be with Mittens. If the raccoon did find out something, he would meet Hunter back there. Hunter ran down the alley and didn't look back.

Twenty-Seven

Hunter didn't have any time to waste. His fear was that he had left Mittens alone too long. She was a good mother, but even a good mother, alone, scared, worried about the future of her kittens, could do something regrettable. He doubled his pace. When he reached the entrance of the den, he was cautious that no humans saw him enter.

He could hear the humans, but he couldn't see them. They were hidden by the wrecks that surrounded the clearing. He slipped into the den. "I'm back," he said.

"So are the humans. I can hear them."

"As long as they stay up there, and we stay down here, we're safe," he said.

"And our kittens, our first brood?"

"They're gone. I think they have been caught in the cages. It's because of the boy, Taylor."

"But why, why would he do that? Why would he take our children? I thought he was good."

"So did I," Hunter said.

"I should have listened to you. You knew humans were bad."

"Not all. The girl who used to scratch behind your ears…she was good. How are the newborns?"

"They're as good as they can be."

"You're a good mother," he said.

"And you're the best father." She reached over and licked him behind the ear. "I'm worried about one of the kittens," she said.

"One of the kittens? Is he not feeding or—"

A loud human scream, female, echoed down the hole and into the den.

"What is that?" Mittens asked. "What's happening?"

"I don't know, but I could go and—"

"Hunter!"

A voice rumbled down the hole and into their den. It was the raccoon.

"Hunter, are you there?" he asked.

"What's happening?" Mittens said. "Are they coming to get us?"

"No, it's my friend, the raccoon. He said he'd bring me information. Don't worry."

Hunter started up the incline. The raccoon was at the top. His head was inside the opening and he was digging, trying to get down the hole.

"What are you doing?" Hunter cried.

"I'm trying to get into your den so we can talk, but it's too narrow." He stopped digging, but his head remained partway down the passage.

"What was that scream?" Hunter asked.

"It was a human. I almost ran into her on my way here. I startled her. She jumped up onto the top of a car like she was a cat. But I have to tell you something about the cages, and about Taylor, what he said."

"You talked to him?" Hunter asked.

"I listened to him."

"What did he say?"

"He mentioned you, Hunter. He wants to find you."

Hunter shivered. "He wants to find all of us," he said. "He wants to trap us, but why?"

"I think he's trying to help you."

"If he wants to help me, he should leave me alone," Hunter said.

"You know I can't understand much of what they say, but I think Taylor wants to bring you all to safety. He asked me to take him to you."

Hunter suddenly realized the raccoon was marking the entrance to the den.

"You have to leave before he finds me!" Hunter yelled.

The raccoon lifted his head and turned to face Hunter. "It's too late. He's standing over there, watching."

There was nothing to do but retreat into the den and hope they were hidden in the dark. Hunter had one thing he had to know before he retreated.

"Do you trust him?" Hunter asked before he retreated. "Do you think Taylor really does want to help us?"

"It doesn't matter what I think," the raccoon said. "It may not even matter what *you* think."

"Then what *does* matter?" Hunter asked.

"What's in your heart may be the only thing that matters. Not what you know, but what you feel and believe. Sometimes you just have to trust."

"And sometimes you have to *not* trust," Hunter said.

"Sometimes," said the raccoon. "But I have to go now—they're coming."

The raccoon pulled his head out of the hole and light filtered down. Hunter retreated into a corner of the den.

"Is everything all right?" Mittens asked.

"Yes, but we need to stay silent. Completely silent."

"But—"

"Silent!" he hissed. Instantly he felt bad. "Please, we just need to stay quiet. It will be all right."

There was the unmistakable sound of human feet above their heads and then Taylor's voice. He was talking, saying things Hunter couldn't quite hear. But he heard his name.

At the bottom of the tunnel, safely in their den, Hunter and his family were silent.

A beam of light shot into the den. Hunter averted his eyes from the brilliance. The darkness of the den had turned to day. Hunter moved to protect Mittens and the kittens, but the beam was too strong and the light filled the space.

Hunter could hear the two humans. Their voices sounded like cats hissing. They were disagreeing about something. Suddenly the beam of light disappeared and the cats were thrust into darkness. It took a while for Hunter's eyes to adjust to the darkness. One of the humans left, but one remained.

Taylor's voice came down the tunnel. It was soft and gentle. He said Hunter's name. Hunter strained to try and hear what Taylor was saying. But he knew humans could lie with their voices, words and even the expressions on their faces. There was only one way he could tell Taylor's intentions. Hunter started up the tunnel toward the entrance.

Taylor kept talking, his voice growing louder as Hunter came up and stopped just short of the entrance.

Taylor was leaning over with his face practically on the ground. Hunter strained to see his eyes. It was so hard, almost impossible. The outline of his head was clear, but the features of his face were hidden by shadows. Taylor continued to talk. His voice was soft and gentle. And then he stopped, and Hunter heard him walking away.

Hunter returned to the den.

"Is he gone?" Mittens asked.

"I think so, but he knows we're down here."

"You have to go! You have to leave before he comes back!"

"I can't leave you behind."

"You have to go! You have to save yourself. Please, leave us. We'll be, we'll be—"

"You and the kittens would die without me. You need me, and I need you," he said. "You don't understand. It's not just that you can't *survive* without me. I can't *live* without you. We stay together."

"But what are we going to do?" she asked.

"Do you trust me?" he asked.

"With my life," she said.

"Then you have to trust me now. I know what to do."

Hunter nuzzled against her. "Trust me." He reached down and took one of the kittens in his mouth. Gently holding the little ball of fluff by the back of the neck, he started up the tunnel.

Twenty-Eight

Hunter hesitated before exiting the tunnel. He was acting on faith and trust—trust in a human. He tentatively walked into the clearing. The humans were there. They were close but far enough away that he could still escape if he needed to. Hunter eyed them nervously. He could always run away, but there was only one way out for Mittens and the kittens.

He walked over to one of the cages. It was empty except for a piece of meat in the center. The smell drew near. The food had lured all the other cats into the traps. They hadn't known any better. But he did.

He circled around the cage, looking for the opening.

He leaned his head inside but kept his body on the outside. He knew what he was doing. If it trapped him, then Mittens and the other kittens would die without him. He was prepared to sacrifice his own life, but not his family's. He had to do this just right. He had to do what only a cat could do.

He leaned in ever so slightly. If he moved too close, the cage would shut. The humans had trapped his other kittens—taken them away from him. He had to trust and have faith in Taylor. And love. Love for his kittens and his mate. He lowered his head and dropped the kitten in. It was done. Right or wrong, it was done. He retreated, the kitten calling after him, desperate and afraid. Hunter felt awful. He was abandoning his kitten, betraying the trust Mittens had placed in him. He slowed down. He could still go back, grab the kitten and...no, he couldn't. He had to trust and follow his heart.

He rounded the corner of the wreck, and the last of the humans disappeared, hidden by the cars. He raced down the tunnel and into the den.

"The kitten, where is our kitten?" Mittens said.

"He's alone. I have to bring one of his sisters to him."

"But—"

"I can't explain. There isn't time. You nurse the other two, and I'll be back."

He grabbed a kitten in his mouth. Every instinct in Mittens, the good mother that she was, wanted to attack Hunter, stop him. But she didn't.

Hunter ran up the tunnel and into the clearing. The humans were still there, watching silently. He had no time to waste. He ran back to the cage. The first kitten's weak calls were the only sound. Hunter stopped at the opening. He had done it once. The second time should be easier. Keeping his feet on the red crushed brick, Hunter leaned in and dropped the second kitten beside the first. Now both kittens began to cry. He ran away, trying to ignore them. He was half finished.

"I'm back," he said as he descended the tunnel.

Mittens was lying on her side. The two last kittens were beneath her, nursing. She didn't answer, but he could hear her panicked breathing.

"Now you have to come with me," he said.

"I'm not leaving my kittens!" she snapped. Even in the dim light he could see the fur on her back rise. She was ready to fight him.

"You're not leaving the kittens. We're taking them with us. I'll take this one and—"

"No!" she screamed.

He was startled by her reaction. He tried to calm her enough so she could follow his directions.

"No," she said, this time softly. "I'll take that one. You take the other."

She stood up and took one of the kittens in her mouth.

"Whatever happens," he said. "You have to trust me. You have to believe in me and what I'm doing."

Mittens nodded.

"Good." He grabbed the remaining kitten, started up the incline of the tunnel and she followed. He broke into the light and turned to watch her emerge. Her eyes were wild with fear. Gently he placed the kitten on the ground.

"Just follow me. Trust me. The way I trust you," he said.

He picked the kitten back up and started toward the clearing, toward the cage. When they entered the clearing, he walked straight up to the trap. This time there was no hesitation in his actions. He dropped the third kitten in with the other two. The three of them huddled together.

Mittens had stopped on the edge of the clearing, terrified. Hunter doubled back and they touched noses.

"Whatever happens we're together," he said. "I won't leave you. I won't let you down."

He led her to the cage. The kittens' cries increased as she neared. Hunter had counted on them calling out for her. They were the bait, drawing her closer and closer.

Mittens stopped at the entrance. She was one of the few colony cats who knew about cages.

Hunter bumped against her and pushed her toward the opening. She resisted. "I know what happened the last time you were in a cage. You lost your claws. But remember what happened to me. Taylor has never done anything to harm us. They *healed* my injured paw."

She looked at him. "That's right. They can heal a paw." She jumped into the cage, the kitten in her mouth, and the door slammed shut. She was trapped inside with her kittens. She was safe; they were all safe. A blur of fur shot toward Hunter. Hunter jumped to the side. King smashed into the side of the trap, pushing it backward, and Mittens screamed.

King turned, but before he could move, Hunter jumped on him, digging in his claws and teeth. King roared in pain and anger. He tried to strike at Hunter, but Hunter easily dodged his blows.

"I'm going to kill you!" King snarled.

"You can't kill what you can't catch," Hunter said. He raced away, circling around a second trap and ran right inside. The door slammed shut behind him.

King stared at him, too shocked to know what to say.

"You're nothing more than a bully. You were never a leader," Hunter said.

"Maybe I'm not a leader, but I'm on the outside of the trap, and you're on the inside."

"You are on the outside, but not just of the trap."

"Fool," King said. "You're as good as dead."

"I'd rather die for something I believe than live for power and greed as you do."

Hunter looked over. The vet was approaching, slowly. In his hands was the long pole, the one he'd used to capture Blue. King's eyes were filled with rage.

"You better run while you can," Hunter said.

"Do you really think you're in a position to threaten anybody?"

"Not me, him," Hunter said and gestured.

King turned and saw the vet.

"Your time has passed," Hunter said. "But stick around if you want."

King bolted, disappearing into the wrecks.

Despite what he had said to King, Hunter was neither confident, nor calm. He was terrified. He wasn't scared for himself. He was worried about Mittens and the kittens.

"I'm right here," he called to them. "Just be calm."

Taylor started to walk toward Hunter's trap and then stopped. The raccoon waddled across the clearing toward Hunter. He pressed his nose against the mesh of the trap, and Hunter did the same.

"You did the right thing," the raccoon said.

"You think it's going to be all right?" Hunter asked.

"Of course. Every direction is the right one."

"I just wish I knew," Hunter said.

"You'll know soon enough, but remember Taylor has never harmed you. I don't think he's going to harm you now. Have faith."

"What else do I have?" Hunter asked.

"Sometimes you don't need anything more. Goodbye, my friend," the raccoon said.

"It might not be goodbye," Hunter said.

"It's at least goodbye for now."

"Perhaps we'll meet in another life," Hunter said.

"Perhaps. And maybe you'll be a raccoon and I'll be a cat," the raccoon said.

"I'll look for the smartest cat there ever was."

"And I'll look for the wisest raccoon." He paused. "But right now I might look for King and have a *word* with him. Perhaps I'll give him more than a word."

"No, please, leave him alone. Even *he* deserves to live," Hunter said.

The raccoon smiled. "You *are* wise. You'll be a good leader. Remember to lead."

There was a loud scream. The man with the cloth on his head came running into the clearing. Hunter's blood ran cold. Something bad was about to happen.

Twenty-Nine

Everyone froze. The raccoon was the first to move. He waddled away as quickly as he could, but then he stopped. He and Hunter locked eyes and nodded. In that brief glance there was respect and thanks.

The man with the cloth continued to scream, and the other humans scurried around the clearing.

Taylor rushed over to Hunter's cage and picked it up. Hunter looked into his eyes. Taylor looked frightened. Were the dogs coming back? If they were, he knew Taylor would fight them off again.

There was a loud hiss and Hunter recognized the voice. It was Mittens. The cage holding her and the kittens had been picked up by the vet. She was snarling, hissing and striking against the cage.

"It's going to be all right!" Hunter yelled. "He's not going to hurt you or the kittens!"

She continued to hiss, but she stopped swatting the cage. When the back of the van was opened, the noise from the other cats was so overwhelming Hunter turned away. It sounded as if the cats inside were being killed. All of them cried out, asked for help, pleaded to be let out of their cages. They were desperate and afraid.

The vet placed the cage with Mittens and the kittens in the van. Taylor handed the vet the cage with Hunter. He moved to put the cage down on the other side of the van, away from Mittens.

"No!" Hunter screamed. "Put my cage by my mate!"

Taylor said something to the vet, and he put the cage next to Mittens. It was as if Taylor had understood Hunter's plea.

The door to the van slammed shut, and the colony cats jumped. Hunter scanned the other cages, looking for his older kittens. Some of the cats were clawing at the mesh, screaming, their eyes wide with terror. Other cats were motionless, almost catatonic with fear. Hunter called out.

"I'm here, Papa, I'm here!" one of his kittens shouted.

"We're all here, all of us," another one said.

"We're scared. Help us!" a third said.

"It'll be okay," Mittens said.

Hunter turned to her. He hadn't expected her to be calm. She was lying down in the cage, nursing.

Several cats screamed in protest and said they were all going to die. That started more cats screeching. The van's engine started, and the rumbling created a moment of silence. And then the colony started howling even louder.

Hunter moved to the side of his cage to get closer to Mittens.

"Come here, please," he said.

She stood up and pressed against the cage.

"It will be all right," he said quietly.

"I know," she said.

"You do?"

"Yes, because you told me."

"We'll all be together," he said. "You and me and our older kittens, and the new litter and…" He was looking at the kittens. They were crawling, trying to get back to their mother. Something wasn't right about one of them. It lagged behind the others and didn't seem to be able to walk properly. It kept tumbling over. Had it been hurt in the move?

"Is something wrong with that kitten?" he asked.

Mittens reached over and grabbed him by the scruff of the neck, pulled him over and put him down with his siblings. "Nothing, there's nothing wrong, not much, nothing that can't be fixed."

Hunter focused on the little kitten. He was black and had a little patch of white on his head. He was definitely his kitten. Maybe he would grow up to be a great hunter. But his front right paw was curved over, or…no… it wasn't there!

"His front paw," he said.

"He has *three* paws that are perfect," she said.

"But one of his front paws is missing. A cat with only three paws can't live."

"No, you're wrong," she said. "He can live. I feel his heart pounding and—"

"He can't hunt. He can't catch food. He can't survive."

"He can survive," she said. "I've seen a dog that only had three paws, and it was fine."

"That was because it had humans to take care of it," he said.

"We have humans here. They can fix it, the way they fixed your paw."

His paw hadn't been missing, it had been hurt. But there was no point in saying any more to her. Not now, not while she was in another cage and he couldn't comfort her or stop her from doing something in desperation.

"What's going to happen to us, Hunter?" one of the colony cats nearby pleaded. Cats all across the van screamed out the same question. Each more excited, more scared than the other. Their desperate cries got louder and louder.

He wanted to tell them he didn't know what would happen, but that wasn't what they needed to hear.

"We're all going to be fine!" Hunter called, trying to silence them. But it was useless. "The humans are trying to help us," he said.

"By putting us in cages?" an old she-cat demanded.

"They put us in cages to help us."

"Then tell them *not* to help us. Tell them to let us go!" she screamed.

"They'll let us go soon," he said. He hoped he was right.

"How can you be so sure?" another cat asked.

"Trust me…trust them."

Their cries continued. Hunter lay down, his body pressed against the mesh. All they could do was wait. And hope.

Thirty

The van lurched to a stop, and the cats swayed forward or crouched, trying hard to keep their balance. Each time the van started forward, they all lost their footing. The cats were exhausted. Hunter looked from cage to cage. Some of the cats were so still, he'd started to wonder if they had died. Then he would see a twitch or a deep breath being taken. He worried about his half-grown kittens, but he soon learned he didn't need to be. They were taking this all as some sort of grand adventure. They knew their dad had been in this van before and lived.

Most of Hunter's attention was focused on Mittens. She was calmly lying on her side. The newborn kittens were pressed against her, protected and nursing. He thought he should be comforting her, but more and more her presence comforted him.

Hunter had been in this van twice before. Neither time had been this long. At least he didn't think so. He knew he had a limited sense of time. When something good happened, it seemed like the goodness had been there forever and would go on forever. When something bad happened, he had trouble believing the torture would ever end.

Every time the van stopped, he thought they would be let out. And each time it drove off again, his heart sank. He had to remain calm, brave and confident. He had to keep the other cats' confidence up.

"When we get out," Hunter said, loud enough for the colony to hear.

"Don't you mean, *if* we get out?" an old tom asked.

"I said when, and that's what I meant!" Hunter snapped.

"You seem so sure of yourself for a cat in a cage," the old tom said.

"I am sure," he said. "When we get out, we will have a meeting to discuss our new colony."

"Is King in here?" somebody asked.

"Not King, he was too smart to get caught," another cat chipped in.

"You're wrong," Hunter said. "He wasn't smart enough to get caught. He won't be there when we start our new colony."

"Maybe we can go back there once they let us loose," the old tom said.

"There won't be anyplace to go back to. King and any cats that remained are as good as dead once they build the new human dens," Hunter said.

The van slowed down and came to a stop. Cats bumped up against the sides of their cages and cried out. Hunter didn't react. Soon, maybe not this time or the next or the next, but soon they would open up the back of the van and let them out.

Among the chorus of howling cats, Hunter noticed something was missing. The van was silent. They hadn't just come to a stop, the engine had shut off. He could hear the humans. They were worried. He wondered what would worry humans?

When the humans stopped talking, Hunter heard the van doors open. Then the back door opened, and light and air streamed in. Within seconds, the humans started grabbing cages. The cats cried, hissed and batted at the cages as they were pulled outside.

"It's going to be okay," Hunter yelled. But he could hardly hear himself.

Cage after cage was pulled out until finally the one containing Mittens and the kittens was picked up. She was still lying down, with the kittens underneath her.

"I'm fine," she called to Hunter. "Don't worry!" he heard her say before she disappeared from view.

He pushed against his cage. He felt so helpless, so scared, but not for himself. Within seconds, before the worry had a chance to sink in, his cage was grabbed and he was hauled outside. Struggling to stay on his feet, he bounced from side to side until his cage was set down.

He pushed back panic and excitement. His body pulsed. He looked around at the other cages. Some of the cats were wild, scratching at the mesh, bouncing against the bars or pacing around their cages. Others weren't moving at all. He couldn't see Mittens, but there were so many cages and some were covered.

Taylor appeared. Hunter was sure that if he watched Taylor, he could find Mittens. The vet pulled away a cover and picked up a cage. It was Mittens! He handed the cage to Taylor.

"I'm here!" Hunter called out, and Mittens looked over. She was scared, but she was still lying down, with the kittens beneath her.

Taylor walked away with Mittens and the kittens. Hunter watched. He tried to focus, keep their scent present even after they were no longer in sight. But there were so many new smells.

Hunter started screaming, "Mittens, can you hear me! Where are you? Answer me! Answer me!"

Taylor appeared once again. But he was carrying an empty cage! Had he let Mittens and the kittens free? He put down the empty cage and approached Hunter. His voice was soft and his eyes were friendly. All the other humans were running around, but not Taylor. Taylor was calm. Hunter couldn't be calm.

"Where are my kittens, where is my mate?" Hunter asked.

Taylor picked up Hunter's cage and started carrying it in the direction he had taken Mittens. He took Hunter to an area where there were lots of cages. Many of them were empty. Others contained cats too confused or tired or traumatized to leave their cages even with the doors open.

Then he saw Mittens! She was in her cage with the kittens, still nursing them. Hunter saw that the door to her cage was open. Taylor put Hunter's cage down beside her.

"I'm here, Mittens, I'm here!" he called.

She glanced up and nodded.

Hunter looked at Taylor and they locked eyes. He wanted to tell him how grateful he was, but he didn't have time. Taylor opened his cage, and Hunter walked right out and then into the cage with Mittens and the newborn kittens.

"We're almost there, it's almost over," Hunter said.

"I knew I could trust you," she said, and they touched noses.

"And I knew I could trust Taylor. We have to get the kittens to safety."

Hunter reached down and gently picked one of the kittens up in his mouth. He stepped out of the cage and looked around. Everything was different—the smells, the landscape, the feel of the place. Then he saw some holes. Could they be dens?

Hunter trotted over to the first hole. He hesitated at the opening. Was another animal still using this as its home? He inhaled deeply. There was a very faint cat odor, but it was from long ago. Nobody had lived in this hole for a long time. It smelled damp. It wasn't going to be a dry home. He walked over to another hole. Again, there was the scent of cat, long since gone, but this hole smelled drier.

Hunter descended into the hole. It angled down gently, not unlike their previous home. With each step, the air became warmer, leaving behind the chill winter weather. He came to the bottom quickly. It wasn't that deep, which meant potentially it wouldn't be that warm, but it was snug. It would do. He placed the kitten down, and she started to cry.

"Don't be afraid," he said. "I'll be back."

He returned to the surface. All around were other cats—some hiding in the rocks and bushes, others out in the open, and others were still in their open cages. Many of them cried out, asking questions, desperate for answers. They saw Hunter as the only one who could help them. But he didn't have time for them right now. He raced over to Mittens and climbed into the cage again.

"I've found a new den," he said. "It isn't as nice as our last one, but it'll be our new home. You need to take a kitten and follow me."

He grabbed a second kitten and she took a third. Mittens hesitated. She felt torn between the kittens that were going and the one left behind. He cried out for her. She knew she couldn't wait. She had to trust Hunter. She stepped out of the cage and followed him.

Hunter stopped at the edge of the hole. He could hear the little kitten at the bottom, crying for her mother. He waited for Mittens to reach his side and then he entered the hole. He placed the second kitten beside the first. Mittens pushed past him and placed the third kitten with his litter mates.

"It's not that big," he said.

"That means it will stay warmer. It's perfect, perfect for two cats and their four kittens."

Four kittens. He knew what she was trying to say. But she was wrong. How was he going to say what needed to be said?

"Do you still trust me?" he asked.

"Of course I trust you, even more than before," she said. "I trust you with my life and the lives of our kittens."

"Then you have to trust me one more time. It's just that, that…"

"I know," she said. "I know." She pressed against him, her nose pushing against one of his ears. "You'll do what needs to be done…for our kitten."

"We have to have faith," he said. "Trust."

He started up the hole, leaving Mittens behind with the three kittens.

At the surface, he was bombarded with cries and questions from other cats. Most of them had left their cages. Some had even taken shelter, but others seemed too stunned to move.

He walked over to Mittens's cage. The last kitten was crying desperately and tumbled as he tried to move. He looked at the black kitten with the little white dash on the forehead, just like his. The kitten stumbled forward, searching for his mother and mates.

Hunter leaned in to the cage to grab it. Instinctively he started for the hole, for Mittens, and then he stopped. He turned and walked toward Taylor.

Taylor didn't move. Behind him some of the other humans had gathered. A wave of anxiety shot through Hunter as he approached Taylor. He stopped in front of Taylor, and they looked at each other. Hunter's fear lessened.

Hunter placed the kitten on the ground and he started to cry. He was afraid and vulnerable without his mother. The kitten tried to get to his feet, but he tumbled onto his face.

"Thank you for everything," Hunter said with his meows, hoping beyond hope that somehow Taylor understood.

Taylor bent down, so that he and the cat were almost eye to eye. Hunter saw nothing but friendship and honesty in his eyes. And in that brief second, any doubts Hunter had about what was to come next were gone.

Hunter picked up the kitten and took a few steps *closer* to Taylor. He rose up on his back legs and rubbed his head against Taylor's outstretched hand. Taylor smiled. Hunter dropped down to all fours, and then gently placed the kitten in front of Taylor. He looked up and the two—cat and boy—locked eyes again.

"You've done so much already," Hunter called out, knowing Taylor couldn't really understand him, but they were words he needed to say. "I need you to do one more thing. Care for him, care for my kitten, keep him alive. If you can fix him, fix him. If you can bring him back to us, bring him back to us."

Hunter turned and walked away.

"Hunter!" Taylor cried.

Hunter turned and looked back, but he didn't stop. He hurried off, leaving the kitten and his cries behind. He stopped when he reached the edge of the opening, where Mittens and the other three kittens were safely hidden.

He saw the vet scoop up the kitten. Fear shot up Hunter's spine. No, he isn't for you, thought Hunter. But the man handed the kitten to Taylor. Taylor looked at the kitten and back to Hunter. The two connected one more time, eye to eye, and nodded. Taylor said something that Hunter couldn't hear, but he knew everything would be okay.

"I know you'll look after him. I trust you," Hunter said and entered his new den.

Author's Note

As with my previous book, *Catboy*, this book was edited and revised with the help of students across the Toronto District School Board.

Every Monday morning for eight weeks, students across the Toronto District School Board received between twenty and twenty-six pages of a new, untitled manuscript. They each read a section and decided what they liked, what they didn't, what made sense and what they wanted changed. They would then email their feedback to me, and the book was edited and rewritten according to their suggestions. While I am listed as the author, *Hunter* had hundreds of student co-authors.

My thanks to the students and staff of Toronto District School Board who contributed to making this novel happen.

ERIC WALTERS began writing in 1993 as a way to entice his grade-five students into becoming more interested in reading and writing. At the end of the year, one student suggested that he try to have his story published. Since that first creation, Eric has published over seventy bestselling novels and has won over eighty awards. Often his stories incorporate themes that reflect his background in education and social work and his commitment to humanitarian and social-justice issues. He is a tireless presenter, speaking to over 70,000 students per year in schools across the country. Eric lives in Mississauga, Ontario, with his wife and three children. For more information, visit www.ericwalters.net.

Will Taylor's plan to save the cat colony work?

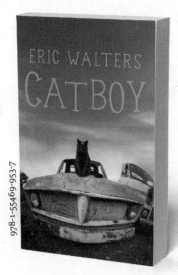

ERIC WALTERS
CATBOY

978-1-55469-953-7

Taylor and his mother have moved from a small northern town to the heart of Toronto. The differences are dramatic as Taylor becomes part of a classroom of kids as diverse as the city itself. While taking a shortcut across a junkyard with his new best friend, Simon, Taylor becomes aware of a colony of feral cats that makes the junkyard its home. Assisted by his classmates, his teacher and the security guard, Mr. Singh, Taylor takes a special interest in caring for the cats. When Taylor discovers the junkyard is being redeveloped to become condominiums, he worries about the cats' survival. Will Taylor's plans to save the cat colony work?